The fierceness of that silver gaze was too much to take head-on.

Heat surged in her head, cascaded all over her body. Her face had to be radiating a red as deep as her hair by now. Her eyes escaped his, only to stray over the rest of him, and—wow! Everywhere she looked, every detail of his striking features and awesome physique—and the thoughts they provoked—were even more blush-worthy.

But something was wrong here. Very wrong. Besides feeling like a derailed train, she felt as if she knew him—as if she *should* know him.

Then it struck her. Hard, then harder. With the force of a jackhammer right upside her head.

No wonder she felt she'd known him all her life.

She had…

Dear Reader

I've always believed heroes are not born but made. I also believe heroes don't know they're heroes—not even when others insist on it. This lack of self-satisfaction is what marks a true hero for me. Vidal, my hero, never suspected he was one—even feared he was the reverse. Both he and Cassandra, my heroine, started out in a wrong place in life, but worked unstintingly to become the best people they could.

I love to explore the life path of people who better themselves, people I can cheer for, fear for, and find total satisfaction when they get the happily-ever-after they deserve. I loved going along for the ride as Vidal and Cassandra made life-changing adjustments and discoveries, and struggled with their prejudices and misconceptions—about themselves and each other.

I hope you will enjoy the ride too.

Olivia Gates

Recent titles by the same author:

EMERGENCY MARRIAGE
DOCTORS ON THE FRONTLINE

AIRBORNE EMERGENCY

BY
OLIVIA GATES

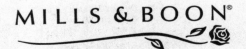

MILLS & BOON®

For my father. The power behind my soul,
the vision behind my being. You live on in me.

First published in Great Britain 2005
Harlequin Mills & Boon Limited,
Eton House, 18-24 Paradise Road, Richmond, Surrey TW9 1SR

© Olivia Gates 2005

ISBN 0 263 84283 5

Set in Times Roman 10½ on 11 pt.
03-0105-54188

Printed and bound in Spain
by Litografia Rosés, S.A., Barcelona

CHAPTER ONE

"OF ALL names, my new boss had to be a *Vidal*."

Cassandra St James winced. She was talking to herself out loud, sounding like a hissing cobra, no less. No wonder the woman ahead of her in the queue had given her that funny look.

What was really funny was that just his name still raised her hackles this way. Brought every sort of fierce nastiness she thought she'd outgrown bubbling to the surface again.

So their mission leader, the man they were transiting in Madrid Airport to pick up, was blighted at birth with 'the name'. Him and a million other men in Spanish-speaking communities. *Her* Vidal was an Arroyo Martinez. He must be in some hyper-advanced surgical center, performing million-dollar esthetic miracles. Her new boss was a Santiago, and he was devoting three months to a grueling, payless humanitarian mission.

She shook her head, paid for her breakfast, tossed her mane of curls back. Better focus on something else. Her life's much-needed new direction, for example. That began today. Her plans to explore new medical frontiers, to break the monotony and the dead ends, were in motion at last. And from the way she saw—saw…

Eyes. Steel and silver. They slammed into her across the huge, bustling cafeteria and held her prisoner. Wouldn't let her look anywhere else. Not even at the face they belonged to.

Her heart lurched and the next scheduled breath just wouldn't come.

Whoa! What was that? She didn't do that. Didn't do instant overwhelming attraction and X-rated thoughts. Or delayed ones, for that matter. Didn't go hot and gooey when a man looked at her. And the man was *just* looking at her.

OK, so no one had ever looked at her that way—ogled her blatantly, sure, especially since she'd set foot in this land of self-appointed Latin lovers—but this...this *devouring* was something else altogether.

People passed in front of her, blocking her vision, severing the connection.

Oh, thank you! She made use of the time out, reached one of the elegant plate-glass tables, swore softly when she splashed cappuccino over her French pastry.

Don't look. She did. She had to, to find out just what that bolt of chemical reaction was all about. Bodies still blocked her view. Then suddenly she had a clear shot of him again and...he was no longer on the other side of the cafeteria!

He was cutting his way through the packed crowds, head and shoulders above other people. Coming to her. Oh, wow!

Her mind stuttered to a standstill as his purposeful stride eliminated the gap between them, then kicked off again, in a jumble.

He was going to talk to her. He *wanted* to talk to her. Oh, yes! But what would he say? What would *she* say? She must look hideous. Her hair was a worse-than-usual mess. Not even lip gloss. She must still be puffed up with that horrible deathlike sleep on board the plane—not that those lethal eyes said anything, but—

A bloodcurdling shriek went through her like a scythe.

Cassandra jerked around, but not before she saw his eyes snapping from consuming to concerned as they refocused behind her, searching out the source of distress.

The shrieks continued, rising to a manic pitch. People were running, some away from the source of disturbance. That added to her confusion until she remembered where they were. In an airport screams might easily be interpreted as some sort of danger. Her first impulse was to rush to help. It must be all her medical training, and probably her knight-to-the-rescue genes as well.

Shouts in many languages echoed. She made out enough to know there'd been an accident. Someone—a child—was injured, unconscious.

She was running by now, towards the milling crowd. *He* was ahead of her, his growls cutting a clear path to the victim in seconds.

It wasn't as easy for her. The crowd closed up again in his wake, didn't part for her as it had for him. She had to shove and elbow away layer after layer of onlookers, trying to get to the object of their horrified fascination.

Her shouts of, "Let me pass. I'm a doctor," didn't make any impression on the predominantly Spanish audience. Then she heard his voice again, snapping something in Spanish, and suddenly she had a front-row view of the emergency.

A hysterical woman being restrained, dragged away. A motionless boy on the floor, or at least a head of golden hair. The rest of him was obscured by the man's huge crouching body. He was already administering CPR.

She groaned. So the boy had arrested. If the man could judge that. And he'd volunteered to resuscitate him—probably on the strength of a technique picked up from some medical TV drama.

Falling to her knees beside him, she tapped him on the shoulder. "*Señor?* I can take over while you make sure an ambulance is on its way. I'm a doctor."

He withdrew to deliver cardiac compressions, didn't even look at her. "I got that already."

She started. His voice—a bass rasp that was just as potent as the rest of him. Concise, cultured. And American. American?

Later. Focus! "Great, so if you'll just…" Her eyes fell on the boy's face before the man swooped to deliver another breath and the words stopped in her throat. The boy's mouth—it was burned!

Fighting off the wave of horror that years of handling the worst medicine had to offer hadn't eradicated, Cassandra's eyes darted around, summing up the situation. A boy of less than three. A pretty plastic tree a few feet away with dangling electric toy planets. They'd been glowing minutes ago. Not any more.

The boy must have bitten the electric cord to pluck one off.

Her stomach heaved again. The center of the burn encompassed both lips in a two-inch, grayish-white, depressed area: the current's point of entry. Electrical burns were far worse than thermal ones as the current arcing through the tissues damaged everything along their path down to the bone. This one, when it healed, would look awful and result in horrible complications, from mouth contraction to tongue adhesions to bone involvement, causing everything from disfigurement to drooling to speech impairment.

But she was way ahead of herself here. No point worrying about those burns now. Keeping the boy's circulation going and oxygen reaching his brain was the number-one priority. She'd better take over and make sure the kid got the best chance. This guy might have taken a course in resuscitation, but young children needed a totally different resuscitation protocol than adults. What would be perfect technique for an adult, or even an older child, would crush the boy's chest with the hard, two-handed compressions, or burst his lungs with the forced ventilation. Even if he knew enough not to be too forceful, he would probably not know that the 80 compressions and the 16 breaths per minute of the usual CPR would be too few to make any difference.

"Sir..." The man withdrew from a breath and she noticed his technique for the first time. It shut her up again.

One large hand pressed down with rapid, shallow compressions. She counted them—at this rate, they'd be an optimum 120 per minute. The other hand had two fingers locating the right position on the sternum, just below the nipple line. The five-to-one ratio of compressions to breaths resulted in 25 breaths per minute, delivered with just the right force. Everything done to the letter of advanced life support protocols for a child that age.

No—not TV-trained after all. This man knew what he was doing. And then some.

Feeling redundant all of a sudden, she fell back on her heels, taking stock, her heart itching at the idea that the man was adding further injury to the mutilated tissues every time he delivered a breath into the boy's inert lungs. Not that that could be helped.

The mother's wailing filtered through to her from a distance. What she must be feeling—the sheer horror and despair! But, then, she hadn't been watching her little one closely enough and she... Cassandra's censorious thoughts stumbled, hot shame squashing them.

Look who's being holier than thou, she thought. Safeguarding kids every minute of the day was one of life's impossibilities. She could vouch for that. What about the right-on-his-head dive Aaron had taken out of his crib, in front of both Amanda and herself? Luckily, he had been OK. No thanks to them.

Her focus returned to the crisis. So the man was delivering first-rate CPR. Working with the presumption it would prove effective, she should assess the boy's other injuries—other burns, any limb angulations. The generalized muscular contraction the jolt must have caused could have been violent enough to fracture bones.

The next second, coughing brought her out of her absorbed examination. The man's coughing.

Still coughing yet not missing a beat, he looked up and she again felt as the boy must have felt the moment that devastating current had arced through his body.

"You a real doctor?" he panted.

Her mind was shut down, but her smart mouth must have been on auto. "No, I'm just a surgeon."

He came up from the next breath with the banked fire in his eyes flaring, promising sensual retribution. *Later,* they said. Now he only rasped, "OK, Dr Surgeon—take over respiration."

She swooped down for the next breath, cringing at having

to bear down on the boy's burnt lips but forcing herself to form a tight seal over his mouth. The man immediately set up a perfect rhythm of compressions with her, then went into another coughing fit.

"Good thing you're here," he gasped once he'd brought himself under control. "No reason to inoculate the kid with more of my resistant strains."

OK, not just a highly trained bystander, then. That was doctor-talk.

"That is," the man added, his voice dipping lower, "if we manage to save him."

Cassandra's heart lurched. "We will!" she gasped after the last breath.

"Hold that thought." He looked up at one of the men standing above her and fired rapid Spanish at him. The bystander rushed to get his cellphone out of his jacket pocket then, following his directions, called a number and placed the phone to his ear. He shot out a string of what sounded like commands into the phone, then nodded to the man, who removed the phone and placed it back into his pocket.

Curiosity overwhelmed her. Who had he called? And how come he sounded perfectly American one moment then clearly Spanish the next? No time, and no breath left to ask. From then on they resumed their efforts in silence, snatching eloquent glances every time she raised her head from a breath. At least, she thought they were eloquent. She felt they were exchanging their gratitude for sharing the massive responsibility with each other. Admitting their strong attraction.

She could also just be hyperventilating.

But she hadn't been when that bolt had hit her a few minutes ago. All right, so she *had* been hit by bolts like that before. But she hadn't been a thirty-year-old then. Merely a stupid teenager who'd just discovered her sexuality and had gone about picking the most disastrous choice to be the focus of her infatuation...

Rushing feet announced the paramedics' arrival, breaking into her untimely musings. How long had it taken them to make it here? And who had the man called? She'd lost track of time, felt as if she'd been fighting for the kid's life for a day—drowning in *his* eyes all her life…

His curt words brought her back to the crisis. "Get a bag-valve mask, a cardiac monitor, the defibrillator, and cut his clothes!"

Yes, definitely a doctor. And he wasn't relinquishing their victim to the paramedics' care. Good—she wasn't about to either. She was seeing this through.

"But it's been over fifteen minutes, and if he's still in arrest—" one of the paramedics started, but the man cut him short.

"I started CPR almost immediately."

"But still…"

"Did no one report he'd been electrocuted?"

That stopped the paramedic's arguments. In electrocution, since the heart had no underlying disease causing the arrest, resuscitation should continue for far longer than for any other cause of arrest. There was always hope an electrocuted victim could revive after protracted resuscitation efforts.

She delivered one last breath before snatching the bag-valve mask from a female paramedic's hands, sealing it over the boy's face and beginning positive pressure ventilation with 100 per cent oxygen. The man stopped the cardiac compressions to attach the cardiac monitor's electrodes to the boy's chest.

Following through with her ventilatory assessment, Cassandra grabbed a stethoscope and listened to the chest. "Chest rising well, equal air entry over both lungs."

The man nodded, finger on the boy's carotid artery, eyes on the monitor. He added his own assessment. "Still pulseless, though—heart's in ventricular fibrillation." He turned to the paramedics. "Charge the defibrillator."

In seconds they'd handed him the paddles of the defibrillator.

"Everyone, clear!" he shouted.

The first shock produced no change in heart rhythm.

"Increase the charge," he ordered.

A second then a third shock still produced no effect. And three shocks were the limit at a time.

"Back to CPR, then," Cassandra said. "Time for venous access and intubation."

"Yes." He made way for the female paramedic to take over cardiac compressions. "Which do you want to handle?"

She didn't relish the idea of coming near the boy's mouth again. "I'll take venous access."

He held her eye for a second, jolting her yet again. He understood her reluctance—sympathized?—With a nod, he turned to the other paramedic. "No. 2 Miller laryngoscope, straight blade, 4.5 endotracheal tube, uncuffed."

Whoa! Not just a doctor. A specialist of some sort. An anesthetist maybe? Whatever, the man was just too impressive altogether...

Drool over him later. Get a line into that little boy.

He finished the intubation, slipped the ETT in place, tested its correct placement and decompressed the stomach to further aid ventilation. Everything done with staggering speed and precision. It didn't make Cassandra feel any better about her struggle to locate a vein.

"No luck?"

She bristled at his question, brought the spurt of irritation under control and made one last attempt. No go.

"Let me do that." He reached out to take the cannula out of her hands.

She turned on him. "You got a way to inflate his collapsed veins?" His eyebrows rose at her vehemence, his hands, too, in a conciliatory gesture. "You go ahead, then," she muttered. "Administer epinephrine though the ETT. I'll go for the intraosseous route."

That hard, hot energy he emitted spiked, the explicit awareness in his eyes back in full force. Still, when he talked, he was the personification of professionalism. "0.2 mg/kg epinephrine, 1/1000 solution," he ordered the paramedic.

Her heat rose. Her concern, too. "0.1 mg/kg is the maximum initial dose via ETT!"

"No."

"Just no?"

"Yes."

Overconfident, imperious. She hated that in men.

"I assume you do know what you're doing?"

"I do."

And she really believed he did. It was probably why overconfident imperiousness looked good on him.

She turned to the paramedic. "You have an intraosseous kit?"

"No, but we have spinal needles," the paramedic said.

"Close enough. Get me an 18-gauge needle." The efficient man handed it to her in two seconds flat. "Ready Ringer's lactate solution, two bags, and giving sets while I do this."

She located the point of insertion in the boy's tibia, an inch above the medial malleolus in his foot, inserted the needle perpendicular to the bone with a screwing motion until it 'gave' when she entered the marrow cavity. A centimeter in, she stopped, removed the needle, leaving the catheter in. In seconds she had her line secure and fluids pumping into the inert boy.

"Good job. No extravasation?" her resuscitation partner asked, checking whether any fluids were leaking out of the bone. She shook her head and he said, "Better deliver the subsequent doses of epinephrine via this route, then."

They did that and after a minute he sighed. "There's a slight change in rhythm—no palpable pulse, though. We'll have to shock him again."

They went through the three-shock routine again. With the last shock, the cardiac monitor blipped the hoped-for change.

"He's back." The man's expression didn't reflect the relief in his voice. Her anxious eyes jerked to the cardiac monitor to make sure. "Sinus rhythm, 80 beats per minute. A bit slow, but we have him back.'' He reached out a hand and squeezed her shoulder. ''Good work.''

Relief and pleasure at his praise, at his touch, melted her tense face into a wobbly smile. One he didn't return, the intensity back instead. His eyes went to her lips, rested there until they began to swell, open—then he turned to the crowd and said something in Spanish. Something about *la madre*. Telling them to allow the mother back? Cassandra had forgotten all about *her*. He hadn't. Nice...

Then everything crashed back on her after the vacuum in which she'd been suspended, with only the man and the boy for company. Even the paramedics had been faceless tools of assistance. Now everything seemed to zoom into existence once again. Bystanders. The wailing mother. Then a second set of medical personnel materialized on the scene.

The man jumped to his feet, exchanged rapid conversation with one of them, and suddenly she was shoved to the side. The frantic mother hurled herself at her toddler, people again restrained her, the newcomers descended on the scene and implemented the protocols of moving a critically injured victim with total efficiency.

Then just as suddenly, the whole crisis receded, leaving her behind.

He was leaving her behind!

He was walking away with a man who probably was the pediatric intensivist who was taking over the case, deep in conversation. Not looking back.

In seconds all she could see of him was the back of his regal head receding out of sight as the sea of people between them thickened then obscured her vision.

As anticlimaxes went, this one was a whopper.

But what had she expected? What was there to expect? They were both waiting to catch planes that would probably take them to opposite ends of the earth. The best they could have had was an hour of—of what? And, anyway, what could possibly top what they'd just shared: dragging a life back from the brink of death? Anything from then on *would* have been an anticlimax. Never had she shared such an intense experience with anyone. At work she collaborated with others, saving lives, daily, but it had never been this immediate, this synergistic.

Now he was gone and the whole incredible experience was over.

She straightened, delayed reaction hitting her. It was already as if nothing had happened, the scene reverting to what it had been previously: busy morning traffic in an international airport.

So, what to do now with enough leftover adrenaline to power her for a month? How to stop it from turning on her, making her legs dough and her nerves exposed wires?

Sit down before you collapse.

Though *that* wasn't such a bad idea right now. It might bring him back, then he would…would…

For heaven's sake! Would what? What was wrong with her? She'd never reacted this way to a man before. Not since…

Her thoughts screeched to a halt again. So did her racing heart.

He was coming back.

His eager stride was eating up the space between them, as if a tape had rewound, snipping out the footage of the last explosive half-hour, resuming time at the moment before they'd heard that scream.

Now it was exclusively personal again, the fierceness of that silver gaze was too much to take head on. Heat surged in her head, cascaded all over her body. Her face had to be radiating a red as deep as her hair by now. Her eyes escaped his, only to stray over the rest of him, and— Wow!

She'd definitely missed a lot during the crisis. Everywhere she looked, every detail of his striking features and awesome physique—and the thoughts they provoked—were even more blush-worthy.

This was getting surreal. After Steve and Daniel, not to mention Rick, she wanted a man and a man's attention like she wanted incurable acne. Anyway, they were passing ships in the night—or planes in the morning—and when it came to looking and fantasizing, she was all for handsome men. And this man wasn't…

No. It would almost be an insult, calling him that. He was…one of a kind. Unadulterated power and maleness in human form. And now she knew the package housed as formidable a brain, his appeal shot to an all-new high. Appeal? Ha! What a lame word to label the jarring response he was wringing from her.

But something was wrong here. Very wrong. Besides feeling like a derailed train, she felt as if she knew him, as if she *should* know him.

Then it struck her. Hard, then harder. With the force of a jackhammer right inside her head.

No wonder she'd felt she'd known him all her life.

She had.

He was *Vidal*! Despicable, mercenary, cold-blooded, self-serving Vidal Arroyo Martinez. The man whose very name had been anathema to her for the past fourteen years. The user, the deserter. And that was just for starters.

He was really here. This was really him. Of all coincidences, of all places. When just an hour ago she'd been cursing her luck that she had a boss with the same first name, memories of him had come back to disturb her more than they had in years. Had the intensity of her antipathy summoned him or something?

Whatever, he was here. And he was now no more than a foot away, coming to tower over her, almost touching her. Then touching her. His thigh against her hip, his hand going to her arm, smoothing it up and down. Familiar, forward. Then his mouth was against her ear, his whisper penetrating her brain, turning it to mush.

"Miss me?"

Her heart kicked, turned. Recognizing him wasn't making any difference, was it? His virility was overwhelming her senses, overriding her mental aversion. She should make some comeback. Cutting and condescending.

He talked first, his eyes sweeping her face, her body, until she felt he'd touched her all over. "I missed you."

The exaggeration hit all her indignant spots. "How could you miss me? Apart from handling the emergency together, we practically haven't met yet!"

"Oh, we've met all right!"

So he remembered her?

"We don't need formalities. Even without sharing the emergency, which can't be topped as introductions go, we met the moment our eyes did."

Oh, boy. So this was the legendary Vidal in action. The world had turned so much, the day had come when she was on the receiving end of his devastating seduction technique. It shouldn't be having any effect. She knew all about him, was onto his every heartless trick.

What *should* be and what *was* had nothing in common.

Oh, why did he have to sound like that? Had he always sounded like that? Opened his mouth and poured out those deepest, darkest vocal caresses?

She didn't remember. He'd barely ever talked to her, if at all. The silent type he'd been. Not any more, it seemed.

He was going on. "Sorry I had to leave you like that. Had to discuss the little boy's continuing care with Miguel, my assistant, about his oral burn, arrange for his follow-up and future corrective surgery. He thought it was incredible for both of us to be here, just in time to help. I think it's more than incredible."

"You think so? I bet you there are dozens of doctors floating around the airport. If it hadn't been us, it would have been another couple of people."

"Maybe, but what about us—before the emergency?"

She was already busy groping for theories to explain her shocking reaction to him, for why he'd singled her out.

He wasn't giving her time to think. "Come on, let's go somewhere where we can...talk." He tugged gently on her arm, his arm going around her shoulders until he had her in the curve of his body, steering her away from the crowds.

In a minute she found herself towed into a VIP lounge, two security men holding the door open for them. Inside there were just three other people, very distinguished-looking men in thousand-dollar suits.

So the man had clout. Didn't hesitate to throw his weight around. It figured. From his more than shady beginnings, he'd always been an opportunist, bent on climbing up as high as he could reach in the world. Over anyone. Years ago, when she'd finally stopped following his progress, and had made sure no one told her any more about him, he'd already reached the top.

He turned from closing the door and bore down on her. ''I came back running, though I knew…'' Those long, strong fingers, his precise surgeon's tools, went to her hair, tucking it behind her ear, the motion intimate. Penetrating. As if he'd touched her in all her secret places. Blood whooshed in her brain, amplified by the sudden change from the hubbub of the open airport to the lounge's soundproofed serenity. ''I knew you'd wait for me.''

She sat down on the plush couch before she fell, and looked up at him as he came to stand above her.

He'd changed. As a young man he'd been incredible. Now…now he was a fully matured force of nature.

No wonder she hadn't recognized him.

Broader, leaner. Tougher. Harsher. And those eyes—no wonder she hadn't recognized *them*. She'd never really seen them behind the obscuring glasses he'd never taken off. Those were now gone. As was the raven, unruly mane, the sallow tinge of years of study and sun deprivation and the yucky facial hair of the last six years of their…relationship. Now he was all silver-laced uncompromising crop, deep bronze and clean-shaven slashed lines.

He'd changed all right, for the best. Only on the surface, no doubt. She'd bet good money the inside changes were for the worse.

If *that* was possible.

Another thing had changed: the way he looked at her. At their last meeting, he'd looked at her as if she'd been a human-sized parasite. Now the look in his eyes said...plenty.

It also said he still didn't recognize her.

The Vidal Arroyo Martinez she had known would have rather been skinned alive than be within a five-mile radius of her. Let alone hit on her.

Ooh, but this was just too delicious! Her anonymity was a great weapon at the moment. No way was she passing up the chance of using it. Let her see how far he'd go if she played this game his way. If she gave him as much rope as he needed to hang himself with.

Her heart was still thumping hard enough to shake her, but her old imp had resurfaced. A dizzying mixture of resentment and excitement drove her on. She fluttered her lashes at him, the exaggerated huskiness in her voice only half pretense. "And as I did, what do you intend to do with me?"

Surprise invaded those annihilating eyes. Though it was followed by a flare of raw hunger, she saw her response had thrown him. He hadn't expected her to be as outrageous as he was.

Oh, yes. Revenge was going to be so sweet.

CHAPTER TWO

"Do YOU really want me to tell you? Or shall I surprise you?"

Vidal heard the aroused tone of his voice, felt his body hardening even more, had no control over it at all.

What was happening to him? What was he doing?

Instead of gulping down some coffee and heading for the plane he should have boarded an hour ago, he was waxing poetic, all but pouncing on the woman. A woman whose name he didn't even know. A woman who might even be engaged or married.

His eyes darted to her hands—those supple, skilled fingers, made for taking lingeringly into his mouth...

Whoa. Focus, Vidal.

No rings. Good. *Great.*

But why great? Why should that matter? In an hour he'd leave, never see her again. And, anyway, she'd said she was a surgeon. That probably explained the absence of rings. She wasn't wearing any kind of jewelry at all. And she should— she should wear sapphires, like her eyes—and nothing else, with just his leg thrown over hers for cover...

What was wrong with him? He didn't pursue women. Never. Not even in his mind. In fact, he'd turned dodging them into an art. So what was he doing, standing there like a hormone-ridden adolescent, panting over this—this...*vision*?

Vision? The woman wasn't even beautiful!

No, just the answer to his every taste and fantasy.

"So, *will* you tell me? Or will you just stand there and hyperventilate?" The vision was also all but laughing her head off at his eagerness. He should mind. He didn't.

20

He gazed into her disarming eyes and something warm and soft spread in his gut. Let her make fun of him if it would keep them radiating that wicked innocence, make that exquisite head tilt, letting that burnished carmine hair riot over those full…

That's it. He'd gone over the edge. Right into mental breakdown.

He'd thought he'd been suffering from clinical depression. But no depression manifested as uncontrollable lust and a desire to make a fool of oneself. Maybe manic depression?

Oh, whatever. It was worth it. *She* was worth it.

"I am far from back to normal." He pitched his voice lower, throwing himself into this weirdness of wanting to be open, needing to communicate. "And right now I'm wiped out. I forgot how exhausting CPR can be. If it wasn't for you taking over ventilation, I think I would have passed out. So I *could* say that's why I'm hyperventilating. But I won't. It's you. You leave me breathless." He reached out, ran his thumb over the elegant line of her nose, tracing the soft freckles' pattern. She let him, her eyes turning turquoise with… equal eagerness?

"And you'll leave me in suspense? Oh, the torture!" she gasped in perfect damsel-in-distress mode, her lament both intentionally silly and provocative.

Her teasing tickled his all but forgotten sense of humor. *Madre de Dios*, she was inviting his intimacy—and what an invitation. Heat rose inside him, took him over.

"Want to know what's torture?" He placed his arms on both sides of her, bore down on her. Her fresh scent deluged him, mock-distressed lips just a breath away. She only deserved that he devour them. His eyes moved from her lips to her eyes, explicit with his desire. Then he voiced it. "Another minute without tasting you."

Her eyes flickered, her lips opened on a tiny gasp. Then her breath rushed out, scorching his cheek. Would she back off?

She didn't.

Purpose settled in her bewitching eyes. Those smoldering, exuberant, piercingly intelligent eyes. Eyes to drown gratefully in. But was that challenge, too? Conviction that *he'd* back off?

Not on her life. Or his. He was out of control, and loving it. Only one thing mattered: showing her how much she affected him. Taking this to the next level, right now. He wanted this to continue, wherever it took him. Wanted to connect with her, bind her somehow, so he'd find her again when he returned.

He sat down on the couch beside her, his hands reaching for her, stinging with the need to make contact with her. Her eyes shot wider before her lids fell, obscuring her reaction. Her head was a perfect fit cradled in his large palm, angled for his deliberate approach. Her heat rose to meet his, igniting him.

It had been too long. Forgotten—no, unknown. That blast of awareness, that gnawing anticipation. He was still alive after all.

His other hand dipped in the curve of her waist. *Dios*— that steep, firm curve. She gasped. He drew her closer until her breasts brushed his chest. Her every nerve seemed to tremble and buzz under hands that felt like electrodes of a monitor, tapping into her reactions, recording them. Turbulent, anxious, feverish. Or were those his sensations, doubling back up his awareness pathways?

His eyes scanned for signs of apprehension, rejection. None. She was nervous, yes, but willing, impatient for him. As he was for her, for those lips.

At the last second, he remembered. His lips landed on her velvet cheek instead. "You got enough of my resistant strains today," he murmured against her flesh, burying his hunger in a trail all the way down to her pulse, settling there and feasting. *Dios*, this was hot, powerful—unprecedented. She lurched, panting as hard as he was. It was the same way with her. "*Querida…*"

"Cassandra, there you are!"

The voice drowned his whisper, snapped their surroundings back. He turned vexed eyes around, saw a brunette walking up to them.

"Thought you must be going crazy, looking for this. Apparently not." The woman held up a handbag, but her eyes were on him. He almost groaned at the familiar combination of extreme female interest and curiosity. "A woman gave it to me. She'd seen us together earlier, said you'd left it behind in the cafeteria when you ran to the emergency. She'd also seen you...rushing here. Sorry I mucked it up a bit. I had to produce something to prove to the guards it's yours."

Vidal still heard the woman talking, yet made no sense of anything any more. The name 'Cassandra' was sinking into his mind like a megaton depth charge. Then it exploded.

Cassandra.

She was a Cassandra? As in Cassandra St James?

No. No. Dios, no! You can't be this cruel.

Thoughts screeched, frantic for a way out, until something started burning inside his head.

It had to be someone else. The world was full of Cassandras.

Si, ciertamente. Full of Cassandras who were American, surgeons, redheads and in Madrid Airport at the same time Cassandra St James was.

And God didn't have anything to do with any of this. He had only himself to blame. He had felt something cataclysmic brewing the moment he'd seen her. Felt it and disregarded it. Chose to misinterpret it even.

But this—this was far worse than anything his morbid imagination could have conjured up.

It *was* her.

Arthur's daughter. Arthur's *daughter*.

Not only that but, if memory served, and it did, the most obnoxious creature who'd ever lived. And he'd been making a fool of himself over her. Far more than a fool. Totally out of line. Totally out of control.

Totally out of character.

Rewind and erase. That was the only way out. Forget his every thought and word and action since she'd turned around in that cafeteria with that pouting glower setting her unique face on passionate fire.

But time travel and rewriting history aside, he just had to resolve the flaming mess he'd made. The poor kid would go into shock the moment he told her who he was.

OK, fine, so she wasn't a kid any more. And she'd never been 'poor'. *Or* a kid, for that matter. The last time he'd seen her, she'd been a pink-haired holy terror. But that didn't mean she wouldn't be shocked now. She hadn't seen him since that fateful day fourteen years ago when he'd come so close to...

Anyway, she'd probably forgotten he existed. Now, when she found out who exactly it was who'd been coming onto her, hot and heavy, who'd had his hands, his lips all over her—*Dios*, would she believe he hadn't recognized her?

Breathe. Snap out of it. He couldn't take refuge in shock any longer. His hands were still around her. Limp and nerveless but still there. He had to remove them, had to look at her some time. At last he did. And what he saw in her eyes...

Blood surged to his head, smearing his vision red.

No need to worry about confronting her with his identity.

She knew who he was.

She'd known all along!

This was better than anything she'd expected.

Vidal had gone from white to green to blue. And now purple.

He realized who she was. Realized she was way ahead of him in the recognition department. And he didn't like it. Whoo boy, didn't he ever.

Let *him* taste crushing embarrassment for a change.

Savor his humiliation later. Run and leave him stewing in it. "Oh, thanks, Ashley." She stood up, making one last contact with his arm as he drew it away, and almost collapsed down again. Her hand trembled as she took the handbag, her other hand on Ashley's arm more for support than for steering her away, too. It wasn't that easy to distract Ashley from gaping at Vidal. She tried harder. "And I hope you kissed that lady for me. It would have been a nightmare if it had gotten lost. What would I have done without…identification?"

She wished she could turn to see her jibe's effect. She couldn't. She could barely keep upright, stop herself from collapsing in demented giggling. She didn't need to look, though. Fury emanated from him, coming faster, hotter, bombarding her, sinking into her flesh, giving her a pretty good idea of how he was feeling.

"Someone would have reported it to airport security sooner or later," Ashley said, resisting Cassandra's efforts to move her, her eyes darting from her to Vidal, full of avid questions.

"All personnel of the Jet Hospital heading to Casablanca, Morocco, please, board now at boarding gate number 19."

The announcement was a summons from the heavens. A perfect escape. "See? Even if they had, I probably wouldn't have had time to collect it."

"Of course you would have. They wouldn't have taken off without you!" Ashley's astonished glance all but asked about her walking away from Vidal without a glance. Vidal, the man whose lips had been buried in her neck just minutes ago. Lips that must have sucked dry all her energy and bravado, right along with her sanity.

She had to run. Now. "Let's hurry. No reason to keep everyone waiting."

She'd taken only one step when his voice broke over her. "Everyone can wait while you introduce me to your friend, don't you think…*Cassandra*?"

His voice. Glacial. Hair-raising. Oh, lord. She hadn't thought this through, hadn't thought how this would end. How he'd retaliate. What if he got abusive?

Well, let him try. Then he'd really get exactly what was coming to him.

Puffing out her chest, she turned. And swayed. His eyes slammed into her again, not with instant desire and enveloping heat, but with an overwhelming sense of *déjà vu*. An incensed Vidal, suppressed violence crackling from his every pore, his formidable body a foot away from hers, trapping her against the wall more effectively than if he'd crushed her to it…

Intimidating. She hated to admit it, but he'd been intimidating then and he was far more so now. She hated, too, to find herself wanting to deny any knowledge of his identity. Oh, no. She'd see this through.

"Oh, we really don't have time for that now, Vidal."

He rose. The world shrank. "But we do, *querida*. As much time as we need."

The change in him was spectacular. No passion now. No humanity. This man looked every atom the soulless narcissist she knew he was.

Those eyes will never feast on you again, make you soar. Oh, stop it!

This was Vidal. He'd been faking it all. Handing her a line. And even if he hadn't been, he was the only man in the species she'd condemned beyond redemption.

"Vidal?" That was Ashley, squeaking. "*You're* Dr Santiago? Our mission leader?"

"No!"

"Yes."

It took a heartbeat for his calm answer to Ashley to sink in. Then it hit. This time, when her heart stopped, it felt as if it would stop forever.

Vidal saw Cassandra's reaction, felt it. He'd been counting her breaths, her blinks, the times she'd licked her lips—those lips… Focus. *Focus.* Not on what he'd thought, felt. On who—what she was. What she'd done. What *she* was thinking, feeling.

This was news to her. She hadn't known he was her mission leader.

How come? Could it be…? Hmm.

Maybe this situation wasn't a total disaster after all.

Before any of them could utter another word, the security guards entered the lounge, deeming Ashley had had enough time to deliver the bag and should leave.

Ashley shrugged her disappointment. "We'll meet properly on board the Jet, Dr Santiago," she said. "I'm your mission logistician, by the way."

It took him a moment to notice Ashley's extended hand. He shook it with a calm nod, calmness that was totally artificial, and saw her widen her eyes meaningfully into Cassandra's shocked ones, giving the message, Later. Oh, yes, he'd love to be there "later," when Cassandra explained this whole mess to her colleague.

The moment the door closed behind Ashley, Cassandra sat down again. Fell down, more like. Savage satisfaction frothed inside him. Good. She was as flabbergasted as he was. But she couldn't be as enraged. All he wanted was to pull her up, haul her into his arms and crush her to his… No, no. He had to stop this, squash it. This was Arthur's daughter. He couldn't think of her that way. Off limits. She was off limits.

"Ha ha!"

His eyes narrowed on her. Saw shock receding, challenge replacing it. What now?

She rose to her feet again, hooked her handbag on her shoulder, tossed her magnificent hair. His body, his head tightened. Dammit. Damn her!

"Good one, Vidal. You almost had me there for a moment."

"Which moment would that be? The one before or the one after Ashley set me straight? The one before, I definitely had you—"

She interrupted him, voice and eyes sharp, color high. "Let's not play any more games. You know what I mean. Now if you're satisfied…"

"Satisfied?" He'd never known frustration like this. Recognizing her should have killed his craving. His body shouldn't still be on fire. This was the woman who'd once been a thorn in his side, who'd given him a harder time than his parents and jailers combined. Who'd clearly matured into a bona fide monster. "And I only realized there was a game going on five minutes ago."

"Yeah, but you're quick on the uptake, I'll give you that. You tossed it right back at me. So, now we're even and I have a plane to catch."

She'd decided he was bluffing, was feeling all secure and relieved again.

That's nice, he thought viciously. Now, to string her along or not to string her along? There *was* the score of those ten years she'd just knocked off his life expectancy.

He stepped into her path as she made to hurry away. She couldn't stop in time. His body broke her momentum. He jerked back the moment she did. This was ridiculous, this current that constantly arced between them.

He should just let her go, get his bearings, stock up stamina for a confrontation, let her find him on the plane—take it from there.

No. They had to settle this now, in private. He couldn't jeopardize the mission with personal vendettas. Drawing this out, to get back at her, was also not on.

There was another call to board the Jet. Her eyes turned from wary to anxious to angry in seconds.

"Vidal, get out of my way and go pick up someone else."

"Is this any way to talk to an old friend and your new boss?"

"Since you're neither, I'll talk any way I please. You've had your joke, Vidal. Now move!"

"Don't worry. The Jet won't leave without me. You transited in Madrid to pick me up after all."

"Cute. You could have read that in the papers. There's been enough publicity over the maiden voyage of Global Aid

Organization's first Jet Hospital over the last couple of days.''

He sighed. There was only one way she'd believe him.

He took her arm and towed her out of the VIP lounge, through the special exit connecting it with the boarding gates.

''You've taken this far enough, Vidal!'' she spluttered, yet stopped resisting him when she found gate 19 at the end of the corridor. Her steps picked up speed, thinking she'd escape him there, leave him behind and forget about him and the whole nasty episode. If only. No such luck.

''As far as you took your…prank?'' They'd reached the boarding checkpoint. She flashed her special pass at the woman, the pass GAO issued its volunteers which would get them on and off the Jet in all their stops around the world. The moment she was ushered in she shook off his hand and strode ahead. He let her go. He'd join her soon enough.

He nodded at the woman who insisted he shouldn't even produce his pass. ''You go right in, Dr Santiago. It's lovely to see you again. We've been hearing all about your Jet Hospital project. May I tell you how great it all sounds? Have a safe and productive journey.''

He passed into the tube connecting the airport to the Jet. Cassandra was rooted there, a look of absolute horror on her expressive face.

She'd heard. Now she knew. It should taste good, getting back at her.

It didn't.

He'd been bracing himself for three months in purgatory being in constant contact with her. But suddenly purgatory sounded good. He'd take purgatory.

For now it seemed he was getting hell.

''You're *not* Vidal Santiago!''

Cassandra heard the choking words, realized she'd said them. It was a miracle she could speak at all. This had to be a nightmare. He had to be lying. This woman back there had to have made a mistake. Another victim of Vidal's hypnotic powers.

"We can stand in this tube all morning or we can board and talk about this later." He took her arm and she shook him off again. He sighed. "All right. Here..." He reached into his jacket's inner pocket, produced his pass and held it up inches from her eyes. His photograph, even grimmer than reality, but him. And the name beneath it. Vidal A. Santiago.

"You can't be Vidal Santiago. Your name is—"

"*Was* Arroyo Martinez—both my father's and mother's family names, in the Spanish tradition. I changed it."

"How? When? Why?"

"Through legal paperwork, a few years ago. That's how and when. As for why, I didn't think I owed it to either my father or mother to carry their family names. Satisfied?"

He'd asked that question before, in utmost incredulity. It was her turn to be incredulous. He'd changed his name? How come her father hadn't mentioned that? Did he even know? No, he probably didn't. Oh, he always said Vidal kept in touch with him, always tried to make excuses for him. But here was proof that he didn't. Her father would have known of his name change if he had. And because he didn't, there she was, with Vidal as her boss. She was going to see him every minute of every day for the next three months!

"Oh, no, you *can't* be my boss."

"Well, I am. And, believe me, I share your horror. But the solution to this mess is all in your hands."

"My hands? What are you talking about?"

"If you take the first flight back to Los Angeles, all this will be over."

"Why don't *you* take the first flight to—to Geneva or Dubai or any other scenic location where you usually stay?"

"Because I'm the mission leader. Without me there'd be no Jet Hospital maiden voyage."

"And without me you'd be minus your chief surgeon and second in command."

"I'm willing to give up the luxury of both."

"You know you can't. And I'm not willing to give up this mission just to make you more comfortable."

"You'd be more comfortable, too. And you don't have to worry about the mission. I'll find a replacement."

"You mean you have surgeons of my qualifications falling over themselves to volunteer for this mission?"

"Not really, but—"

"So when do you expect to get someone else? A week before the mission's over? Or do you intend to postpone it until you do?"

"A day's delay costs tens of thousands of dollars…"

"So there will be no postponement, will there? If I leave, you go out there short-staffed, *boss*."

His neutral glance turned dark. Forbidding. She shivered and looked away, refusing to let him see how he rattled her. "So we're trapped, aren't we?"

A moment's silence, then he exhaled. Without volition, her eyes went to his. They'd emptied again. When he spoke again his voice was as vacant. "Seems so. And since we are, let's not make much out of this. It was really too silly. So, whatever you were putting me in my place for, I hope it's out of your system now."

He didn't know what for? He didn't remember? Probably. He must have had a thousand similar incidents in his life. Not that *that* incident had been what had driven her to lead him on. Her loathing had ceased to be personal long ago. She had endless reasons, family-related as well as professional, to despise Dr Vidal Arroyo Martinez, a.k.a. Vidal Santiago.

He didn't wait for an answer. He just turned and walked away. In a minute, he disappeared through the door of the aircraft. Feeling stupid and very, very small all of a sudden, Cassandra followed, reality sinking in with each step.

Please. Let me wake up screaming, in a cold sweat and in my seat.

She didn't. And wouldn't. This was one nightmare she'd have to live through.

"Come in Dr St James," Vidal said when she stood hovering at the door of the cockpit, his voice and his face expressionless. So, that was how it was going to be from now on, huh? She should have felt relieved, but she only ached with disappointment. Losing that fierce hunger that ate her up, made her soar with giddy gratification... "Meet Captain Harry Styles."

Giving herself a mental shake, she shook the captain's hand. Vidal went on. "Harry is our operations manager and the best pilot on planet earth."

The tall blond man guffawed. "That's right, Dr St James. And Vidal can tell no lies."

Nice man. A few years older than Vidal, open, with loads of positive energy. Not like the debilitating electricity Vidal generated. She liked him at once. Her smile warmed, tension seeping out of her. "Cassandra, please. Dr St James is a mouthful."

"With pleasure, Cassandra. Lovely name for a lovelier lady. My opinion of surgeons is fast changing." Harry winked at Vidal.

Some intensity entered Vidal's blank expression as he looked at his friend, yet there wasn't even the shadow of a smile to answer the man's wide grin. The Vidal she'd known hadn't been given to smiling. Come to think of it, he hadn't smiled at her at all so far. Not even when he'd been intent on seducing her. He'd scorched her to the bone with his blatant desire, but no smiles.

"It would have been scary if you found me lovely, Harry." Vidal's dry answer brought another guffaw from Harry. Vidal's lips twisted. She couldn't call that a smile either. "So, Cassandra, I presume you've met everyone?"

She shook her head. "No. I boarded the Jet after a six-hour wait in Los Angeles airport and fell asleep the moment I hit my seat. I woke up when we landed in New York then went right back to sleep the rest of the way to Madrid. I haven't gone over the Jet either. Just studied the schematics and leafed through my job description."

"That's what mission leaders are for. We'll go over everything in detail together, the technical matters as well as the mission specs." Vidal turned to Harry. "How about introducing your flight crew to Cassandra now?"

"Sure," Harry said, and picked up the mike.

She stopped him with a hand on his arm. "Please, no. Let me get to know them during the trip, one by one. If you line them up and fire names at me, they'll just spill out of my other ear."

"Sounds like a good plan." Harry grinned at her.

"Realistic at least," was Vidal's dry rejoinder. "I've met only a few here, too. So, what would you advise, Harry? Should I brief everyone and lay down the ground rules now, or later after take-off?"

"You go ahead now. It'll be another half-hour before take-off," Harry said.

"Call everyone for me, then." He turned those cool eyes on her. "After you."

Smiling a goodbye at Harry, she preceded Vidal out of the cockpit, almost bumping into the man entering it in her haste to move away from him. Murmuring a greeting to Sean McMahon, the copilot she'd already met, she almost shouted for Vidal to keep away from her. But he was away now, a few footsteps from her. Yet his aura was all around her. She finally flopped into her seat, the one she'd chosen in the third row, shaking with relief at having put a few meters between them.

By now, Harry's page had brought the flight's medical volunteers and all other personnel flocking to their seats. Vidal stood in the left aisle, beside the huge screen facing the seating area.

He started immediately. "Good morning, everyone. For those who don't know me, my name is Vidal Santiago. I'm your mission leader and I'm what everyone likes to call a plastic surgeon. I don't know why—I haven't operated on any dolls yet. I prefer the label of reconstructive surgeon, but who am I to argue with common opinion?" He paused as chuckles rose, then went on. "Before I give you a quick run-through of our mission and our facilities, let me thank each and every one of you for being here today. You could have been somewhere else making money, or at least sleeping in your own beds every night.''

He nodded to Louisa, the nurse Cassandra had spent the hours at the airport with, and she handed him a baton and nodded to a flight attendant.

The lights dimmed and the screen lit up, turning Vidal into a towering silhouette. The sight thumped in Cassandra's chest, making it hard to breathe, to understand a word he said.

She tried harder, heard him saying, ''I'm sorry for all the time you lost and the confusion over your roles and the mission's schedule. The mess-up and the last-minute changes are all my fault, I'm afraid. But you have an idea about the mission and now I'm going to use this slide show to recap everything, make the transition from the theoretical to the practical and give you a clear overview of what this mission entails.''

He unfolded the baton to its two-foot telescoping length, rapped it onto his other palm, held it there like a principal addressing his third-graders.

''First, some boasting. No matter what other agencies tell you to the contrary, our Jet Hospital is *the* largest, fully equipped, self-contained airborne hospital ever built. We're a one hundred per cent non-religious humanitarian effort and our mission is unequivocal: we're citizens of the world and the Jet Hospital will be available to help the sick and needy of any nation.'' He paused, then drawled, ''Do inform me if I'm boring you to tears. My bite *is* worse than my bark, but, then, you're all brave people or you wouldn't be here in the first place. No contenders? Hmm—the kind of team I like to lead.''

A ripple of laughter echoed. Cassandra bristled. Mostly because she found her lips twitching, too. So the man had a sense of humor. When had he grown one? Or had he had it grafted?

''OK, after that back-patting we've all yet to earn, let's

get down to some hard facts. Louisa?'' The first slide flicked on the screen. A cut-through diagram of the Jet Hospital. "I'll be predictable and go from front to back. Behind the cockpit, the Jet has the crew transportation-educational center we're currently in, which has a seating capacity of ninety. We're below that number now, but as we land in our target countries and patients and local medical personnel join us on board, we might have to break out the folding beach chairs. I hope you brought your own.''

Another ripple of laughter. He didn't wait for it to die down and went on, commenting on each slide as it came up. "These are the dental, ophthalmology, ENT—ear, nose, throat—stations. Here's the trauma-triage area, the minor surgical-examination area, the pre-operative and recovery area with fourteen hospital beds. And last, in the back, the four surgical suites. Our facilities are state of the art, with the latest technology in diagnostic equipment, laparoscopic and arthroscopic surgical equipment and a complete pharmacy.''

"You mean we have a CT machine beneath all those covers?'' Joseph Ashton, the mission's head anesthetist, whom Cassandra had met briefly before boarding, asked.

"Give us a break, will you, Joseph? We've got everything, apart from CT and MRI machines—space limitations, you understand.''

"And how complete is the pharmacy?'' a man she didn't know asked.

"As complete as they come.''

Get to the important stuff, she was about to scream. She wanted this little reconnaissance over and Vidal out of her sight. And earshot.

"Are we going to talk about the mission details?'' She was aware of everyone turning to look at her. She lowered her voice, injected neutrality in it. "Up until yesterday, there hasn't been a definite itinerary. And what about the case load and distribution of responsibilities?''

He turned his eyes on her in the semi-darkness. Did they glow or was she hallucinating? Probably both.

"After Casablanca we go to Muscat, Oman; Hyderabad, India; Tashkent, Uzbekistan; and Baku, Azerbaijan. As for our case load, those have been preselected by our partnering medical facilities in each of these countries, on the basis of complexity and unavailability of proper treatment options locally. So your guess is as good as mine. Among us we do have enough expertise to handle anything they throw at us. As for responsibilities, those will have to be flexible. Each of you will still be in the position you signed on for, but I'll work out a list of daily chores, then *you* will make sure everyone knows where to be and what to do on each given day."

"Where to be? You mean in the different stations in the Jet?"

"No. To get the most done, whenever possible we'll work in partnering hospitals and offsite clinics, even set up tents in auxiliary areas to treat medical conditions that don't require the Jet's facilities."

"Is the training-teaching side of our mission still on? I heard it was off because of time constraints."

"Then you heard wrong. We will be training local medical professionals in the latest medical and surgical procedures. Either on their turf or on ours, either by direct attendance or tele-medicine—broadcasting on-board surgeries in this miniature theater. There'll be lectures, too, which each of you will contribute to."

A general murmur of unease went through the audience.

"C'mon, folks. Stage fright never killed anyone. Start thinking of the most recent and effective procedures that benefit you in your specialty and write something comprehensive. Anyone needing any reference resources, we have two computers with a complete medical library."

He waited until they settled again. "So…I expect you to get to know one another. Those I haven't met, come later, one at a time, please, and introduce yourselves. Now, problems! When they're medical, you report to me. If I'm unavailable, you report to Dr Cassandra St James. If it's anything else, I advise you run to Harry, or anyone from our management team, consultants or logisticians.'' He stopped, his eyes panning over the crowd. ''Hi, there, Ashley.'' Cassandra heard Ashley's splutter. He moved his focus at once but Ashley's distress didn't end that easily. ''OK—questions?''

No one said anything. What was there to say? He'd said it all.

So the man had rhythm, focus, and clarity of communication. He'd make a hell of an instructor.

He snapped the baton closed and sighed. ''I see I've put you to sleep. Good, you'll need it in the coming months. In fact, I advise you to grab every moment of rest you can. And don't eat anything you don't recognize. We don't want any of you on our patient lists. Anyone interested in going over the Jet for real, follow me.''

The light came back on and she blinked. He passed by her seat, not even looking at her. Her every hair stood on end nevertheless. She rose, followed the line that had formed in his wake. All the women were in that line.

She gritted her teeth. His harem had already formed. The worst part was she knew why. She'd gotten a first-hand taste—and touch and scent—of his influence, hadn't she?

But it wasn't only that roiling inside her. Her mind was tangling over his contradictions. His multiple personalities, more like. Which was the real him? The Vidal who'd rushed to save the little boy, who was heading this most ambitious humanitarian mission? Or the Vidal who'd treated the people who loved him like dirt, who'd made a staggering fortune combining his surgical talents with the tricks he'd perfected through his years as a con artist and a thief?

CHAPTER THREE

"HAVE you made up your mind yet?"

Chocolate cake went down the wrong way. A second later one sound thump between Cassandra's shoulder blades saved her from choking.

"Did I startle you?"

Vidal came to sit beside her and her coughing intensified, tears running down her face. "No, it's a hobby of…mine," she choked. "Inhaling…chocolate cake!"

Dispassionate eyes watched her until she settled down and back in her seat. "Ask a stupid question. Care to answer the one that startled you so much?"

She squinted at him, wiping her tears. "If it made sense, I would."

"I did ask you at the end of our tour of the plane, before take-off."

"You asked if I intended to bring anything personal, real or imagined as you put it, into our work. I already said of course not."

"I know what your lips said, but it doesn't seem your mind is co-operating. You've been close to hostile with me so far."

She didn't answer straight away. His accent was suddenly back. Its absence when she'd first met him had been one of the things that had thrown her off track. Although he'd been born in the United States, he'd grown up in an almost exclusively Spanish-speaking community. He'd had dodgy English until the age of fourteen and an accent until the day she'd last seen him. He didn't any more, but now it was back again. Weird.

"Well?"

"I've been totally professional. And if I made a short comment or two, they were for your ears only."

"You know what big ears people working together have. And living in such close quarters, believe me, they'll be picking up the vibes sooner rather than later. Having their so-called leaders at odds with each other won't be conducive to a good working environment."

"Vibes? Not much I can do if we enter the realm of the metaphysical."

"Just tell me this—what are *you* so resentful about? I'm the one you made a fool of. Just what do you have against me?"

"You really don't know?"

"*Por Dios*, you've always been on my case, even after I got out of your life, and I'll be damned if I know why you hate me so much. Was today payback for that day you suddenly decided I made good target practice for your budding feminine wiles?"

"I don't hate you, Vidal. I don't do destructive emotions. You're not on my list of favorite people, that's all. And, really, today had nothing to do with the incident you refer to."

"The incident? In the singular? I seem to remember a string of disasters. Ending with me drenched in cocktail in my so-called moment of glory, with palm imprints on both my cheeks, two women calling me names I've yet to know the meaning of, accusing me of things I never even imagined, in front of a hundred people. And all captured on video. I even made it to some gossip column. Complete with photographs."

She'd been sixteen and what everyone had described as wild. At least as far as extreme sports, hobbies and fashion went. And she'd been reeling with the discovery of the secret from which her parents had protected her and her siblings so well. It had been Vidal who'd told her, erasing the knight's image she'd superimposed on his true character, rewriting history, her very memories, making her feel lost and agoniz-

ingly foolish. So she'd retaliated. Surely such a big, bad man
could handle being made to look foolish, too?

She'd invited his last two discarded girlfriends to the graduation party her father had thrown for him in their home,
knowing what harpies they were. And he had been there
sporting his latest conquest, the girl who'd taken the state
beauty-queen title from both of them. It had just been a matter of waiting for the fireworks to start. She couldn't have
anticipated they'd be so violent, though.

Things had gotten ugly, fast. But funny, too. The women
had been so over the top, while Vidal had been so immov-
able, so unresponsive in the middle, it had turned into a farce.
Her lips twitched at the memory.

An intimidating sable eyebrow rose in irony. "So you're
still enjoying the joke. The old, or the new? Both, no doubt.
To be expected really. You were always a pain in the—"

"Is this any way to talk to an old friend?" She couldn't
hold back. A chuckle escaped.

"You were right the first time, Cassandra. We were never
friends." His voice was as bored as his eyes. "We stayed in
the same house and you harassed me from the first day I set
foot there until I stopped giving you the chance."

Stayed in the same house? That was how he viewed living
in her *home*, her parents equally his, till he'd walked out of
their lives, never to look back? And "harassed" him? That
was how he viewed her misguided hero-worship? The man
was as cold as they came.

"Then I went and gave you another chance today." He
leaned closer. Not improper close, but she still felt trapped.

Trapped. Like that night of the party. He'd chased her to
her father's study, trapped her against the wall, his muscular
arms on both sides of her head, the bars of a prison she'd
been desperate to escape—desperate never to escape. He'd
stood there above her, the cocktail still dripping from his hair
and glasses, his fury lashing her, everything about him making her weak, dizzy, scared—elated. She'd stared at him, trying to reconcile the image she'd held of him all her life with

what she'd discovered. He'd stared down at her until time had warped and stopped, then he'd sworn in Spanish and exploded out of the room, out of the house. He'd never returned.

"Fourteen years pass and the moment I see you again you play another dirty trick on me. Tell me, Cassandra, is this the only way you get your kicks?"

"Believe it or not, you're the only one I ever played those tricks on."

By way of explanation or peace-offering, that stank.

Those impressive eyebrows rose again, made it clear he agreed with her thoughts. "Oh, I'm honored. But just in case you feel tempted to pull this kind of trick on someone else, remember—most men wouldn't just let it go."

Was he telling her he would? She met his steel eyes. He was. She noticed something else, which had been niggling at her since she'd first laid eyes on him again. Beyond the magnificent looks and the innate power, there was that...depletion, that dimming. He'd said he wasn't back to normal, had been coughing, mentioned resistant strains. He'd been sick, seriously so.

Suddenly the agitated resentment that had had her in its grip since she'd realized his new superior position in her life evaporated. She felt sick with the drain, sick at her behavior. Her behavior had been inexcusable, even before she'd known the full truth. She was being childish now.

It was pure defense. Instinctive, unreasoning. His very nearness fried her self-restraint. Memories of his lips tapping her lifeforce, drinking deep, buzzed in a loop in her mind, scrambling her logic pathways. And she'd thought she'd been laying a trap for Vidal. *He'd* climbed out unscathed.

What had she been thinking? Why had she done it? To punish him—for what? Betraying every ethic and value and tie she held dear? Using his gifts not to benefit humanity but to amass wealth and power? Being indiscriminately promiscuous? Hurting her father, the man who'd snatched him out of hell? Or was it for his continuing hold over her father's heart and, worse, his faith, when Vidal had never done any-thing to earn them, let alone keep them?

Well, here he was, seemingly doing his bit for humanity. His sex life had nothing to do with her. And her father was capable of settling his own scores, and free to love and be-lieve in anyone he pleased—her approval wasn't required.

No matter what she thought of Vidal, personally or pro-fessionally, leading him on had been stupid, not to mention bitchy. If she'd had time to think about it, if she'd been capable of one clear and rational thought back then, she would have probably backed off.

No matter now. It was time to start again. At least try to.

He was getting up, ending this.

"Vidal…" She grabbed his arm. His sculpted, hair-roughened arm. He sagged back heavily and she jerked her hand away.

Stop being ridiculous. Just get this over with.

She took a deep breath. "I was out of line. I should have told you who I was the moment I recognized you. Believe it or not, I didn't recognize you at first either."

His eyes narrowed on her face. This must be how it felt to be hooked up to a lie detector. "You didn't?" She shook her head, mute. His probing deepened. "Then when did you?"

"After you came back from talking to…Miguel, was it? Anyway, what I mean to say is that I *am* sorry. It was stupid and on the spur of the moment, and I would take it back if I could."

Her apology brought something fierce flaring again in his distant eyes. He had every right to be angry. Was he? No anger emanated from him, just…just… Oh, she didn't know. He was too confusing, too opaque.

A long moment later, he lowered his eyes, exhaled and fell silent.

Vidal kept his eyes on his arm, searching with every iota of concentration for the burn mark he was certain her touch had left on his flesh. He had to. Or else he'd haul her into his arms and pick up where they'd left off.

He'd been keeping his senses focused just off her, shutting out the memories.

Then she'd had to go and tell him *that*.

So it hadn't been an act. Every second, every sensation, starting with their eyes colliding, connecting across the cafeteria, during saving the little boy, as he'd rushed back to her afterwards. All real. She'd recognized something in him, known they'd connected on a fundamental level. Up until the moment she'd identified him.

And then? She'd teased and taunted him, hid her identity, led him on, to toss his weakness in his face later. But her eyes, her heat, her scent, her tremors had still revealed her real response. The reactions her mind couldn't override, her will couldn't hide.

Dios, he didn't need to know that.

How could he convince himself now that his helpless reaction was just a misinterpretation of his sense of recognition, too?

Yet maybe the overpowering mutual attraction had been just that, their subconscious minds telling them they knew one another, shared a long, involved history filled with turbulent emotions.

Si, ciertamente. If that was it, he should be sitting straight in his chair now. Just the memory of the wild girl who'd given Arthur, *and* him, nightmares as she'd been growing up should have frozen his libido solid. He shouldn't even have a libido where she was concerned. He never should have.

Maybe he was suffering from his prolonged abstinence? But he hadn't been abstaining voluntarily. He'd just lost interest. Until he'd wondered if he'd ever have urges again, had almost forgotten what it felt like to have them.

So, was he having a backlash of uncontrollable lust now? But why should she be the one to resurrect his desires? *Resurrect?* He'd never had it nearly this bad. All his life women had told him he was one cold son of a bitch, on all counts.

It had to be artificial, this new fire. It was the weirdness of the situation. Or maybe he'd caught *her* fire. No doubt it would soon be extinguished, as fast as it had been ignited.

It had better!

Until it did, he just had to keep it neutral, force himself to cool down, forget. Grit his teeth and walk through the hell of the next three months.

A self-deprecating sneer almost escaped at that. He'd grown soft. This hell should be a breeze compared to the one that used to be his reality, his home.

But he'd escaped his home. There was no escape this time. This was a sentence he had to serve.

It wouldn't be the first time.

Vidal took a deep breath. His lungs itched with the lingering infection that had almost killed him. A lungful of her scent didn't help.

Get it done. Accept her apology, start afresh. Was that possible? They had to try.

"Cassandra, no apologies needed or expected. No more pranks either. Let's just get on with our jobs. I'm determined to make this mission a success. I'm sure you are, too."

"Why?"

What?

His focus sharpened on her face again. Damn. He'd intended to get up, end this right now. It had been a lousy idea, sitting this close to her. Dangerous. This close up, she was overwhelming. Cream and carmine and turquoise. Every line of feature and body detailed in an elegance and voluptuousness the masters had only tried to imitate, and failed. Whatever had happened to the pink-haired, black-eyed, covered-in-freckles, scrawny livewire? Though she'd stirred him even then, so much he'd... Oh, hell!

She'd asked something. Better use the distraction. "What do you mean—why?"

"Why—everything?" Her lids were half-closed, making her eyes thoughtful, curious, their luminescence undiminished by the horrible lighting of the plane. Something fizzed inside his brain. "Why are you here, doing this? Is this some sort of propaganda campaign? A grand philanthropic gesture to add to the Vidal Arro— Vidal Santiago legend?"

"Is that what you think?"

"I don't know what to think. That's why I'm asking."

"It's clearly what you want to think. Go ahead, make yourself comfortable. Believe what you like. Just as long as it won't interfere with our work or you taking orders."

"Ah, we come to that. You're going to enjoy this part, aren't you?"

"It'll be novel, that's for sure. As far as I remember, you never took orders from anyone, never followed rules."

"Gee, you make me sound like some sort of anarchist hippie, instead of a highly disciplined trauma surgeon."

Indeed. It had been a shock when Arthur had told him she'd entered med school. A bigger shock that she'd stayed, excelled. The Cassandra he'd known had made an art of squandering her abilities, superior in everything, sticking with nothing, ending up far behind her peers. When and why had the change occurred?

He shrugged. "*Touché*. So, why yourself?"

"Why am I here?" Her eyes crinkled, laughed, a hundred mischievous imps rollicking there. Something very painful twisted behind his breastbone. "*I'll* be charitable and satisfy your curiosity. You're right. Following rules isn't for me. It has definitely gotten *to* me. I've tried the sedate path of academia ever since I entered med school, then I finished my residency and looked around. Didn't like what I saw. I had nothing to look forward to but what I got a full taste of during my residency—endless surgery lists, patients a thousand other surgeons can help, and step after step up the hospital executive ladder. Not what I envisioned when I entered med school. So I decided to go where people were really in need, where my presence can and will make a difference. I hooked up with GAO and they sent me to Afghanistan for two weeks. And, wow. I decided there and then that this was what I wanted to do with the rest of my life."

"What did your parents have to say about it?"

"I told them only after I'd come back from Afghanistan. I just wish I hadn't told them about that shooting incident. They were so horrified they tried everything to stop me from enlisting for this mission, said I was putting myself in more danger if the Jet visited regions of unrest. Dad asked me to wait until GAO had tested the Jet, tightened the efficiency and security of its missions."

"But you ignored him, of course." As she'd always ignored his worry, his concern—his unconditional love. Remembered bile rose up again. For her to have Arthur and Mavis for parents, while he'd had his. And she'd never even realized how lucky she was! He'd always believed one day with his parents would have cured her, would have had her on her knees first thing every morning and last thing every night, giving thanks for the privilege, the blessing.

"I don't ignore my dad. We discussed his concerns and agreed that no one can predict danger. And what's more, what made me more liable *or* more important than everyone else embarking on this mission?"

"In other words, you bulldozed him as usual, got your own way." Before she could blast him with the retort that erupted in her eyes, he added, "And what did Steve have to say about this? I seem to remember you were engaged?"

"Are you for real? That was eight years ago. You think I'm still engaged to him?"

"So what happened? Did you leave him? Marry him?"

He knew the answer to that, knew the answer to all his questions. He just wanted her version. Hoped to make her uncomfortable. As she made him.

She was far from uncomfortable. Her eyes gauged him, his knowledge of her life events, decided he didn't know much. She smiled. "The first, thankfully. Then there was Daniel then, last and least, just a few months ago, Rick. Another reason I'm here."

The men's names rolled off her tongue, landed in a rocky lump in his stomach. Arthur hadn't told him about those last two. Had there been others? And what did it matter to him if there had been? It didn't! Of course not. Still, the taunt he couldn't curb didn't sound all that indifferent. "Seems you've been quite busy."

She threw it right back at him. "Nowhere near as busy as you. Three guys in fourteen years isn't so bad. But, then, those were supposed to be serious relationships, so I guess we don't have a frame of reference for comparing our track records. You don't do serious. Or even pseudo-serious-while-it-lasts, do you?"

Or at all. But he wasn't about to tell her that. "No, I don't. I work. I have no time and no need for anything else."

"Anything but the...obvious."

Sex. And after the way he'd been all over her, she'd never believe the truth. He raised his eyebrows in a nonchalant expression, avoided replying.

"Do you know, I met an ex of yours a few years back at a party. She had a very interesting description of you: 'a systematic paragon of efficiency and a self-acknowledged emotional void'. She said the void part was a direct quote."

"Don't know about paragon. The rest sounds accurate. If bitter. And I never gave a woman reason to be bitter. If I said those things to her, it had to be as a warning—a disclaimer, if you like. If she chose to disregard it, she shouldn't be blaming me."

"Oh, she must have made the usual female mistake—thought she'd be the one to fill the void, then got angry when she realized there was no filling it."

Vidal's snort was derisive, surprised. Cassandra was good. Acute. Insightful. And so damned plain-spoken. He'd forgotten how direct she was. How invasive. It was getting more dangerous by the second.

Get her mind off probing you.

Harry's voice came over the intercom, announcing their imminent landing at Casablanca's international airport, saving him the effort.

"So, Cassandra, nice stroll down memory lane and all, but

I take it we're agreed. Bygones are bygones, no more surprises, pure professionalism.''

"Sure, boss."

That look in her eyes, that smile. Images spread in his brain, seeped through, hot, deep. His fist bunching in her waterfall of hair, dragging her, his tongue thrusting those flushed lips open, his lips, his teeth sinking into them, leaving them swollen with his brand forever. Then it would get really intense…

Purge those images. Now. Ban them.

"Cassandra!"

"What's with the warning tone? I said 'Sure, boss,' didn't I?"

"Yeah. So why do I suddenly wish you'd said, 'No way, José,' instead?"

She just chuckled and buckled her seat belt. He got up and went to his seat.

He buckled himself in, closed his eyes and struggled with his rampaging senses.

Arthur, why didn't you ask for ten pounds of flesh instead?

"Do you realize *every* patient on our list is a plastic surgery case?"

Vidal turned from inspecting an exam station, his steel gaze sweeping over her. Her heart picked up about a hundred extra beats per minute.

Instead of answering her, he turned again to the three nurses who were assisting him. "Louisa, Martha, prepare the other exam stations the same way. Dick, tell Dr Rodriguez to prepare two hundred X-ray plates. Thanks."

The two women skittered, the man almost did, too. Cassandra closed her eyes, her guts balling into a mass of resentment.

"You were saying?"

"C'mon, Vidal, you not only heard me, you knew this beforehand!"

"Yes, I heard you. And, no, I didn't know. I guess the

moment the Moroccan health authorities and our local spon-
sors learned it was me heading this mission, they decided to
take advantage of the fact and lined up all plastic surgery
cases needing my level of experience."

She'd deduced as much. "That's nice. What are those of
us who aren't paragons of plastic surgery supposed to do in
the meantime?"

"You'll assist me."

"Oh, joy!"

"You had craniomaxillofacial surgery in your multidisciplinary trauma surgery training, didn't you?"

"It's one of my special interests, yes, but—"

"Then what are you moaning about? A lot of the cases
are right up your alley. You said you saw the list?"

"No, just talked to Fadel, our public relations liaison from
Moulay Abu Sayed hospital."

"And what did you assume? That all the cases were *cosmetic* surgery? Rhinoplasty, body sculpting, rejuvenation?"

Yes, she had. "They're what you're famous for."

He inclined his head, his gaze penetrating her to the bone.
"They are?"

"I've seen your miraculous results on more celebrities than
I can count, heard how in demand you are, not to mention
the astronomical fees you charge."

"And you think the mission's organizers decided to forgo
the 'humanitarian' part and are making use of my presence
by sending over Morocco's wealthy in search of artificial
beauty and youth?"

"I don't know, do I? Up until two days ago all the plans
were vague. They still are. I really don't know what to expect."

"Expect this." He handed her the dossier he was holding.
"Bear in mind that those are our partnering hospitals' diagnoses of the selected cases. We'll make our own diagnoses,
then we'll decide whether the treatment is surgical or not and,
if so, exactly what kind. Now, I must organize the next two
weeks with Harry and Fadel. Then I'll hand you the schedule

and expect you to marshal the troops. I also have to see about our accommodation. It's the height of tourism season and they couldn't get enough bookings in hotels near the air-port—I must do something about that.''

''I...'' Cassandra found herself talking to his receding back. In seconds he, Harry and Fadel had left the Jet and curiosity overcame her befuddlement. The dossier! Her eyes went over the pages, speed-reading, her mind sorting out cases by category. Craniomaxillofacial surgery cases—all sorts of cranial and facial deformities, congenital and post-traumatic. Hand surgery cases. Problem wounds care. Oculoplastic and orbital surgery from eyelid tumors to trau-matic and atrophic deformities of the eyelid and orbit. Breast reconstruction after mastectomy.

Not what she'd expected at all.

''Did he tell you when he's coming back?''

She jumped.

''Hey!'' Ashley laughed. ''Sorry I startled you. I just need to co-ordinate some chain-of-supply matters with him and Harry.''

Her heart rate sank back to normal. Maybe she should consider taking tranquilizers for the duration of this trip!

''I don't know, Ashley. And this is a comprehensive state-ment.'' Ashley's eyes filled with the questions she really wanted to ask. Cassandra intercepted her before she voiced them. She also had to amend the answer that made her sound like an uninformed idiot! ''But in the next twenty-four hours I intend to be on top of things. Let's go after him. I need that schedule he promised me.''

Before Ashley could say anything more, Cassandra was out of the Jet, getting her first breath of fresh air in over forty-eight hours.

Ashley followed, turned up her face to the Moroccan November sun. ''Wow, the weather is great! Sure is a lovely change from our freezing climate.''

''Don't include me in this 'our','' Cassandra said.

"I forgot you live in the sunny south. Los Angeles must be about the same this time of year."

"Both cities *are* at around the same line of latitude, but the weather here is…different. The light, the breeze, the very ambience. Something exotic about it. Must be the land, maybe echoes of its Moorish past."

Ashley's brown eyes twinkled with her usual gaiety. "Ah, all that poetry when the airport looks like any major international airport. What will you say when we enter Casablanca itself?"

"Nothing, I guess. I've heard Casablanca is no sleepy dive with latter-day Humphrey Bogarts around every corner. It's just another bustling, modern port and metropolis."

"I refuse to believe that. There must be some mysterious oriental flavors."

Cassandra shrugged. "Let's hope so."

"Think we'll have any chance to go about the town?" Ashley asked.

"Here come our fearless leaders. Let's ask *them*."

Vidal had just appeared around the Jet, with Harry and Fadel and a long line of people, most carrying babies or small children. He topped even six-foot Harry by a few inches. But now the hunch to his shoulders was noticeable, as was the dragging of his feet. A spurt of concern rose in her throat.

Like he needs or wants your concern. Like you should even feel it.

She met his tired eyes as he approached before he switched them to Harry. The moment everyone was on board, Ashley pounced on both with questions and demands. Cassandra left them to it and went to Fadel.

"Did you have to go get our patients yourselves?"

Fadel rolled his eyes. "Airport authorities insisted on getting Vidal's corroboration that indeed all cases require your services."

"Don't tell me he examined them all. You were gone only twenty minutes!"

"It took Vidal twenty seconds to give his OK."

A closer look, a real look, told her why. Every infant and child had a cleft lip, unilateral or bilateral. Whether those were combined with cleft palate was yet to be seen on examination. She'd seen enough of those cases in her early surgical training, had assisted in enough cases herself, to know what a serious condition this was and to regret it was so prevalent. One in seven hundred children was born with a degree of the anomaly, and sometimes it heralded far more serious congenital abnormalities. Even isolated cleft lip and/or palate had severe repercussions if left untreated, from inability to feed to speech impairment to psychological problems.

And though the treatment was a multidisciplinary one, involving ENT specialists, dentists, speech pathologists and pediatricians, it was primarily a plastic surgeon's job. She'd never known that Vidal took the least interest in the condition.

The man in question was coming towards her. Her heart kicked as she now expected it to. "Gather our craniofacial team, Cassandra. Work up a chain of assessment. Divide up patients more than twelve months old between them. Keep everyone below that for me. Call me when you're done."

Without one extra glance, he shuffled away, disappeared into the cockpit. Was he looking worse or was that her imagination? She had to stop herself from running after him to make sure. Had to suppress the absurd worry. He'd given her her first order, hadn't he? Better get down to doing what she'd signed on for!

For the next hour, she sorted the patients, talked to their caretakers in a mixture of English, French and Arabic supplied by Fadel, and gathered the mission's dentists, ENT specialists, their sole speech therapist and every nurse. When everyone was busy examining their patients, she went to call Vidal. She approached the cockpit to the sound of his hacking cough.

Her concern wouldn't be suppressed any more. Finding

him alone, she burst out, "You're not examining those babies, coughing like that!"

He sat forward, bracing his arms on his knees to steady himself. "I won't cough all over them. That's what masks are for."

He thought she was worried about the kids? She should be—but it hadn't even occurred to her. Oh, damn.

Sort out your messed-up priorities later. Now convince him to take some cough sedative, get some rest, leave it to you altogether.

But he was getting up, crowding her on his way out, and her objections evaporated on another heat wave.

Maybe he wasn't the only one who was sick!

Seven hours later, their examinations and preparations for the next day's surgery list over, they were on their way to their hotel, thirty kilometers from the airport along the wide, busy, French-like boulevards of El Dar El Baidaa—Casablanca in its literal Arabic meaning of "the White House". Cassandra didn't have eyes for the delightful public parks and imposing Moorish civic buildings on both sides, only for the man sitting beside her.

Vidal had his head thrown back against his seat, eyes closed. Gray.

What was it with Harry and Fadel? Couldn't they see how ill Vidal looked?

She heard none of their nonstop gabbing until Vidal joined in, his voice a bass rasp, his breathing strident.

"Quit apologizing, Fadel. You did a great job, got us all rooms within half an hour of the airport. Our schedule problems are my fault, not yours."

Fadel shook his head. "I just wish *you'd* agreed to go to one of the better hotels. Here in Maghreb—that's Morocco in Arabic—it's a matter of honor to get the boss the best of everything. And you're all this mission's bosses."

Harry laughed. "Vidal says us bosses should set a good example, scrape the bottom of the barrel, put up with the worst. I don't mind as long as the hotel is rat-and cockroach-free.''

Fadel spluttered—assurances, no doubt. Cassandra only heard Vidal coughing again. Her chest tightened some more in empathy.

Half an hour later they turned into a dingy-looking alley. And there was their hotel. What had she said about dives? By all standards, this was one.

''Ouch,'' was Harry's good-natured comment when the interior more than lived up to the exterior's threat.

Vidal's eyes, hooded and turbid now, were on her. ''Go back with Fadel, Cassandra, squeeze in with a couple of the other ladies.''

''Taking me off the mission bosses' list already?''

''I didn't know it was going to be this bad.''

''It's not so bad,'' she lied. ''And Fadel said he'd get us better accommodations as soon as possible.'' She didn't wait for him to insist, aborted the arguments filling his eyes by walking away, pretending to inspect the Moroccan articles in the gift shop. Soon Fadel came back with a scrawny bellboy, full of apologies, said he'd pick them up in the morning, then streaked out again.

Minutes later, she was leaning on the door of her tiny, dank, single room, every nerve-ending prickling with excess electricity.

Macho Vidal, carrying his bag up the four flights of stairs, trying to carry hers, when he could barely carry himself! Big spender Vidal insisting on lavishly tipping the bellboy himself! Everything he did was just—just— Aargh! Then there was everything else going on. So much had happened today. So much to think about, to puzzle over, to feel—to fear…

Pushing herself away from the door, she forced herself through her nighttime routine.

She was already in bed when she realized she hadn't locked her door. Rushing to lock it, she discovered the key didn't work.

It wasn't hers.

The bellboy had given her Vidal's key!

The idea of making the exchange right now survived for about half a second.

A few minutes later, with a chair jammed beneath the doorknob, she was lying in bed, jumping every time Vidal's coughing carried to her through the flimsy wall.

Suddenly, it built to a crescendo. A racket of falling items followed, then staggering footsteps and a huge thump on the floor, rattling her whole room.

She shot up in bed, her heart hammering violent blows against her ribs.

What was that? Had he fallen?

She froze, shivering with anxiety, listening.

Dead silence.

Even if he'd fallen, he'd get up, go back to bed. She'd hear his movements. She waited a few more minutes, all sorts of noises carrying to her from Harry's room, the whole hotel. From Vidal's side, nothing.

Unable to bear it any more, she erupted from her bed, tore the chair propped against the door aside, ran barefoot over the greasy corridor carpet and banged on his door.

"Vidal?"

No answer.

A violent shudder racked her. He might have hit his head, might be bleeding to death as she stood outside, stupid, useless.

The door is unlocked, idiot! Just get in.

She fumbled the door open, almost sobbing with urgency, almost fell inside.

Total darkness.

And that silence! Oh, lord…

Search for the light switch.

She moved. Her foot caught on something hard. She fell full length, hitting a body on the floor. A still body.

She screamed.

CHAPTER FOUR

SOMEONE had fallen over him.

Someone had screamed in his ear and now lay plastered to his flesh. Still screaming. Not just someone. Cassandra—hot, fragrant. Shaking apart.

He was dreaming.

He had to be. He'd closed his eyes with the sight of her filling his mind, his senses. His dreams must be giving him what he craved. The forbidden things he'd never have awake.

But, if so, shouldn't she be moaning his name in need, not screaming it in terror? Maybe this was a nightmare?

"Vidal!"

OK, so that didn't sound like something generated inside his head. Neither did the feverish hands on his chest, his face, his head feel like the stuff of dreams. They were too real. Too arousing. Too…scared?

Dios, was she in danger, seeking help?

His eyes snapped open to…nothing, absolute darkness. He exploded into motion, snatched her beneath him, his mind refusing to work, every instinct screaming at him to hide her, protect her, shield her.

"Vidal. Oh, God, you're alive!"

What was she talking about? And why was it so dark?

"Vidal, for heaven's sake, it's me, Cassandra!"

Of course he knew that. He'd know her now, blind and deaf. He'd scent her. Sense her. Did she think he'd ever fail to recognize her again? Oh, no. Never again. He remembered how he'd wanted her, how they'd connected the first time, remembered how it had felt. The hot, sweet, painful thickening in his blood, the tug of longing stretching his awareness beyond endurance.

56

"Stop it, Vidal. Are you awake?"

Awake? Of course he was. He didn't sleep any more. He closed his eyes and waited out the nights.

"Let me up, Vidal. Where are the lights in this room?"

No, he couldn't protect her if he let her up. Lights would end everything, expose him.

"Vidal!" She sounded angry now. And it got through to him.

He wasn't dreaming—more like hallucinating. He knew it now.

He willed muscles that felt as if they belonged to someone else to relax. Memories then realizations followed, still as if in someone else's head but clearer now, real.

They were in a hotel. Cassandra was next door. Now she was underneath him.

If only it was for real.

No. He had no right to even think it.

Light. Turn on the light. There had been a lamp above him on the nightstand beside the bed he'd left. He reached for it, flicked it on. Then wished he hadn't.

The sight would haunt him till the day he died.

Cassandra. In his arms, vital, glowing, hair an angry splash across the drab mattress, eyes almost as black as when she'd worn those atrocious contact lenses, lips a deeper red than her tresses, moist, trembling. He knew he shouldn't look any further. He did. Towards the neck he'd suckled, the one he wanted to sink his teeth into now—and beyond. Was that what she went to bed in? Wisps of red silk? Would he ever go to bed again and not see her there in them? Out of them?

Dios, what was she doing here? Had she been sent by some malevolent demon to push him over the edge?

He should get off of her. Remove his thigh from between hers. He moved and only pressed on her harder. *He* couldn't be any harder.

And she must know that, too. The cover and her nightdress between them were no barrier.

Let her up!

He tried to move but didn't have enough leverage. Then she shoved, rolled and fell off the mattress, taking him with her. They lay there on the floor, fused, panting.

Her shudder blazed through him. Her snarl too. "Clever, Vidal. Tell me, were you sure I'd fall for this?"

His mind was working again, sluggish, creaking but working. Should her words make sense?

"Don't even try to look confused. Turnabout is fair play only if you dish it back the same way. My trick was silly. You almost scared me to death. Now get off me."

"Slow down, Cassandra. I'm pumped full of codeine and just can't follow you. What are you talking about?"

"Oh, please!"

Please, what? Give you what our bodies are begging for?

Out loud he said, "I'm totally in the dark here. I only remember the bed creaking every time I coughed, each creak going through me like a quake. I threw the mattress on the floor and collapsed on it. The next thing, you were slamming on top of me and screaming. It took me a while to wake up. I'm still not sure I'm awake."

Her pupils fluctuated, and so did that incredible color of her eyes. With what? Suspicion? Hesitation? Hunger? Or was this another trick?

He was in no shape to work it out. He'd never understood her anyway. All he could do was wait for her to enlighten him.

Cassandra stared at him, her voice gone. She'd found it before in sheer panic, then in sheer fury. But now, if he was telling the truth...

He was! For the first time ever, she could read him. His barriers were down. Confused, disoriented—aroused. Viciously.

Something scorching and giddy surged inside her.

Oh, please! He'd react the same way to any female who threw herself on his bed, moron.

Better worry about *her* reaction. What she saw in her mind's eye. Herself arching against him, offering, opening, begging...

Just what was happening to her? She'd come here thinking he was injured, helpless. Now she knew he wasn't, she should run back to her room, shouldn't be lying beneath him almost fainting with need. This couldn't be happening to her. Not with Vidal!

End this now.

She drew in a ragged breath. A mistake. Her breasts pressed into his unyielding chest, into his heat, his virility. Hair rasped against silk, abraded the nipples it covered. The sound, the feel... "Vidal..." *Kiss me there, anywhere, oh, please, please...*

No!

No. She hadn't said that out loud, thank God. *Focus.* "Vidal." She tried again, hated her wavering whisper. "I assure you, you're awake. And though I'm grateful you're alive, I'd appreciate it if you let me up."

He just shifted so his arousal wasn't pressed into her, yet his arms kept her in place. "Not before you tell me why you're here."

He meant it. But that was as far as she could read into his expression now. He was back to being unfathomable. He'd shut down again.

Her breath was measured this time, just enough not to pass out, to be able to answer him.

"So, all's well," she concluded a couple of minutes later. "Now, I'll take my key, go back to my room and let's try to grab some sleep. Tomorrow—uh, make that today—is a huge day."

He held her eyes for one more moment, then unclasped her, moved away, leaving a cold, aching void along each inch he'd freed. She shuddered, scrambled up. Once upright, she ventured a look back at him, found him sitting up, covers bunched around his lower body, the rest of him naked...

Look him in the eye, don't do this to yourself!

She did, found those eyes on her lips, until she almost felt his lips there too, then everywhere, taking every liberty, driving her beyond reason, beyond self-preservation. She almost swayed back, almost fell to her knees beside him.

Sex. It was just sex.

Oh, there was nothing "just" about it. It wasn't fair that he, of all men, should do this to her. Without even trying.

She turned, her eyes searching for her key, getting desperate.

She heard the rustle of clothes, the sound of a zip, then he was behind her, handing her the key. "You said I scared you to death. Why?"

"Why? Because I thought you'd *died*. I landed on top of you and you didn't even move."

"Why should that scare you? You would have gotten rid of me if I had."

"How twisted can you get? How twisted do you think I am? I don't want you dead!"

"You looked mad enough to kill me yourself when you suspected this was all a ruse."

"If it had been, I would have!"

He huffed something. A laugh? No—just another of his sarcastic, hollow parodies of laughter. "How did you even think *that* a possibility? How would I have known you'd hear the racket I made, interpret it the way you had, let alone come running yourself, instead of calling Harry or hotel security?"

"Pardon me if I wasn't thinking clearly at the time. I'd just had the scare of my life, thinking you'd cracked your head open, then I found you on top of me, breathing hard and not answering me."

"Did I scare you?"

This surprised an emphatic, "Of course not," from her.

The bigger surprise was that he should have. A man twice her size, bearing down on her, clutching her with bruising force, his arousal growing by the second, pressed into her thigh—she should have been at least alarmed. It had never even occurred to her to be.

With a jolt she realized she would have been if it had been any other man. With Vidal, she just *knew*, no matter how aroused he was, that she wasn't in the least danger, not even of a few messy and humiliating moments before he took no for an answer. Not her, not any other woman in the same situation.

How contradictory was that? What had happened to her firm opinion of him as a sexual opportunist, a heartless swine? It seemed her mind thought something and her instincts thought something else. Which knew what it was talking about?

"Glad to hear it. I think I was hallucinating. In a second I created a whole drama around you being here. People were after you, and I had to hide you. Must be the half-bottle of cough medicine I gulped down after we finished work. That must have been why I was knocked out so deeply, too."

Her concern erupted again, in full force. "That's another thing. You're sick and I really don't think you should be working at all, let alone this hard."

"I'm fine."

"Yeah, sure. That's why you've been coughing your lungs out all day."

"Don't tell me you're concerned!"

Was the man for real? She was almost-had-a-heart-attack concerned. Yet, if she could be so incredulous that she was concerned, *he* sure wouldn't buy it. No matter. She had to get him to rest, recuperate. "Don't you think you're taking this doctors-make-lousy-patients bit too far? What were you thinking, taking on such a huge job when you're in such a condition?"

"The mission couldn't wait forever and my illness had messed up schedules already. I'm well enough now."

Suddenly it was imperative to know. "What was wrong with you?"

What was it that tumbled in his eyes behind the steel?

Surprise? Vulnerability? Emotions closed her throat. What if he had something serious?

He folded his arms across his impressive chest, shrugged. "That's a long story, and it's not the time or the place to be telling it."

She was about to argue, unbearably moved, anxious, and totally confused as to why she was. But he *was* looking worse than ever and she wasn't contributing to the recuperation she so much wanted him to have by interrupting his sleep, keeping him out of bed.

"OK, Vidal, later, then. Sorry I barged in like that."

"What are you apologizing for? You saved me."

"You didn't need saving!"

The fierceness that flared in his eyes made her gasp, added to the jumble of confused emotions roiling inside her. He lowered his eyes, eclipsing his expression, his deep voice softening. The world started to blur. "If I'd needed saving, you would have saved me."

"It's the thought that counts, huh?" She tried to laugh it off.

"Absolutely."

"I would have done it for anyone."

Nothing changed about his expression or body language, yet if she'd thought he'd shut down before...! When he raised his eyes to hers again, all signs of life were gone. "I know that. You did it for the man who tops your contempt list."

Twenty-four hours ago his statement would have been met with a resounding, "You got that right!" But now—now she no longer knew anything.

Take those words back. Oh, why had she said them? And said them like that, making it sound like he'd just been another creature she had to help, just on principle? When nothing was further from the truth...

Not knowing how to even start taking it back, she mumbled, "See you in the morning." And ran out.

*   *   *

Vidal sank down on the mattress, too drained to even undress again.

Not drained enough, though. He was still throbbing, his starving senses still snatching at traces of her.

He drowned the room, his senses in darkness again. It made no difference. His mind's eye could see very clearly. Replaying her every nuance, her every expression. Her every word!

What had he ever done to deserve anything she'd ever felt towards him? The fascination or the revulsion?

As a child of three, she'd latched onto him on his first day in her home. Shadowed him, big blue eyes fascinated, fixated. Why, he'd never understood. She'd scared him. He'd only wanted to hide, fade into the background, petrified to draw attention to himself, to do or say anything that would be wrong, that would make Arthur send him away, back to hell. But her focus had put him in the spotlight. He'd resented her for it. Feared her. Yet he'd told himself she was just a kid, to either handle her or evade her.

He'd soon given up on handling her and had perfected the art of evasion. But it had gotten worse with every passing day. She'd gotten wilder, more effective, cornering him. He'd no longer feared her as much as he'd feared the temptation to play the hero she'd wanted him to be. But that meant betraying Arthur, falling from grace. It also meant reaching for something he'd never deserve. There'd been one way out: telling her the truth. Showing her what he really was.

He hadn't expected her to hate him for it. Pity, disappointment, disdain. Those he'd expected, he'd deserved—still deserved. But not hate.

He'd rationalized it, though, had had no illusions. She'd made advances to the man she'd thought he was. Once she'd seen his reality, she'd hated him in retrospect for every moment she'd been deceived about him, begrudged him his luck and Arthur's caring, when he'd never deserved any of it.

She'd invited those women to his graduation party, hoping he'd show the whole world his true nature. He'd almost shown *her*...

Was she still trying to punish him? Didn't she understand she'd punished him enough already? When she'd driven him away from the St James's home once and for all. When she'd faced Arthur with his greatest mistake—picking him off the streets, forgiving him his crimes.

Ten years, and still her words, the ones he'd overheard in Arthur's office during one of his periodic visits to him at work, rang in his ears. Arthur had never repeated her words. But in his eyes afterwards, there had been that regret. It had cut him, deeper than anything ever had. Deeper than the gashes his father had carved in his flesh. For what if it meant Arthur agreed, regretted his kindness?

This morning, her punishment had been far harsher. To let him think he'd finally found someone who stirred him, on every level, only to find out it was her, the one woman who'd never see beyond his flaws, who knew his sins down to the most humiliating, disgusting detail. The one woman who would always be off limits, in every way...

Oppression almost suffocated him. How had he dared to even think she'd worried about *him*? He'd even fished for an admission that her panic had been personal. She'd sure put him straight, underlined how irrelevant he was to her. Just another live body to save.

It took a saint like Arthur to care about the likes of him. But Cassandra...

An image of her lying beneath him, her eyes clouding, her scent thickening with the desire that had shaken her, that she'd fought and hated, slammed into him, left him gasping, groaning in pain.

No, she was no saint.

Dios l'ayuda, neither was he.

"Dick, are you getting us on the screen?" Vidal asked into the microphone clipped to his scrubs.

Dick Baringer's voice crackled over the speakers. "Yeah. ER quality!"

Vidal shook his head. "Weird. We look atrocious on the

monitor.'' He made gesture of a belated, gallant apology. ''Not the ladies, of course.''

Cassandra heard chuckles from the educational center in the front of the Jet, partly directly, partly over the sound system.

Vidal began. ''So, ladies and gentlemen, if everyone's settled in, we'll begin our first tele-medicine session. Welcome on board GAO's first Jet Hospital. It's a pleasure to be forging closer collaboration between us, the medical professionals of the world. I hope you find our visit informative and useful and that our connection will continue beyond the duration of our two weeks' stay.'' Vidal raised his eyes, caught Cassandra's, set the now-expected fireworks in a chain-reaction along her nerves. ''Now, Dr Cassandra St James will give you an overview of our schedule.''

Was his voice as subdued as she thought or was it just the mask muffling it? Why was he wearing it already? Worried about his 'resistant strains'?

No time to worry about that now.

She nodded, started her prepared speech. ''Good morning, everyone. The first four days of our surgical schedule consist of 143 surgeries. Sixty-two are babies below twelve months and the rest range from one to ten years. Cases range from complete unilateral cleft lip to bilateral to a combination of cleft lip, soft and hard palates, from partial to complete. Now, a quick overview of the condition.

''Cleft lip—or hare lip—and palate result from incomplete fusion of the right and left sides of the mouth during the first trimester of pregnancy. The reason is unknown, although there are some genetic theories. It can range from just a notch in the lip to a complete separation of the upper lip, extending to the nose, either on one side or both sides. Cleft palate might or might not accompany it, since both have different developmental origins. Cleft palate ranges from a split uvula to a complete fissure running through the soft and hard palates—the roof of the mouth—forward to include the alveolus—the gum.

"Corrective surgery is preferred before the age of twelve to fourteen months to avoid the development of severe feeding and speech problems, not to mention psychological ones. Still, the ideal treatment involves a multidisciplinary team approach, not just one operation. This team *should* include a pediatrician to oversee the child's development, a general plastic surgeon, an oral maxillofacial surgeon for teeth and palate development, an otolaryngologist for diseases of the ear, a psychologist for both patient and family, a speech and language therapist and a clinical co-ordinating nurse."

"And it isn't even her specialty!" Vidal's approval coursed through her, the flush on her arms telling her that her face must be clashing horribly with her blue scrubs. "Regrettably, our patients today, and all through our mission, are mostly orphans or as good as, and such continuing and co-ordinated medical care as Cassandra outlined is out of the question. There are institutions here to offer them *some* of those services, but we, and each one of you, have to face the fact whenever we're treating someone in similar conditions that staged therapy is a far-fetched dream and that what we do while they're within our care might be the only treatment they'll ever receive. We must make it enough!"

Cassandra's eyes widened. The passion, the determination. Was he putting on an act? If he was, it was an award-winning one.

He was going on. "OK, on to today's cases. I've selected them to be broadcast since they represent the full range of repairs done in cleft lip and/or palate. Tomorrow, the plastic surgeons among you will assist us here, when all four surgical stations will be working simultaneously and practice what you'll see now hands on. Sam..." Vidal turned to the nurse operating the video camera "...pan on the operative field." He kept his eyes on the monitor until the angle satisfied him then said, "OK, fix it. Getting a clear view, Dick?"

"Clear as can be."

"If you're wondering what that is in eight-month-old

Omar's mouth, I'll let Dr Sommers, our chief oral maxillo-facial surgeon, tell you about it.''

Phil Sommers, a blue-eyed, lanky blond man in his late thirties, waved at their audience, his broad smile a tribute to his profession.

"Mornin', all," Phil said in his broad Southern drawl. "Basically, this here is a custom-fitted denture or molding plate and the procedure of placin' it is called nasoalveolar molding. I was sorry to see this li'l tyke was the only one who has had it done among all our patients. The procedure is the best thing so far for preparing for cleft-palate surgery and getting' the best results from it.

"The plate is gradually adjusted to reshape the roof of the mouth, causing the bones of the upper jaw to grow toward each other and the space between the gum pads to narrow. It also separates the oral and nasal cavities, which are open to each other in babies like Omar, with both cleft lip and palate. It also improves nasal support on the cleft side and creates a tunnel that should develop bone after surgical repair so bone graftin' won't be needed. Now Vidal can repair the gum at the same time he repairs everythin' else, with minimum tension, reducin' scar formation and improvin' esthetic and functional result.''

"Another expert who knows his stuff," Vidal said. "Phil will be giving practical workshops in how to perform the procedure every day from 6 to 8 p.m. on board the Jet. Thanks, Phil. Now, I'm going to fix both palate and lip in one procedure which I estimate will last about two hours, so grab your coffees and sit back and watch.''

Vidal had been sitting at the head of the operating table. He now looked sideways at Joseph. "Everything go?" The anesthetist nodded and Vidal looked at Cassandra. "OK, let's begin.''

The next hour was a revelation.

She'd always known that Vidal was good. Hard not to know that with "he's the best" always following any mention of his name. But what she saw, what he was, went beyond good and best. *She* was those, but he was magic. Art of the highest order. Scalpels and scissors seemed to float in his fingers, slicing the baby's flesh but not traumatizing it, healing it instead, restoring it right in front of her stunned eyes. All the time he explained every cut, every lift of tissue flap, every repositioning of muscle. And all the time he demanded her assistance, which she gave him as if they'd been working together every day of their careers. Then she started anticipating his requests, drawing his surprise then his appreciation.

"After elevating those two muscoperiosteal flaps," Vidal explained, as he put the last remodeling touches in the palate before closing it, "I am now elevating, redirecting and repairing the levator muscles." He paused as they finished doing just that. "And here we are—a three-layer closure of nasal mucosa, muscle and oral mucosa. Now to repair the lip."

If he'd impressed her out of her mind working on bone and cartilage, he flabbergasted her working on muscles and skin. He elevated art to virtuosity.

"This is called the Millar procedure, everyone," Vidal explained. "Or the rotation-advancement repair. The principle is simple, as anyone who's ever done any patching work will tell you. Simply put, when I do that…" He cut through the orbicularis muscle, the muscle that formed the bulk of the lips, just below the nose and into the naris. The incision produced triangular shapes on either side when the lips sagged down on release of tension. "I create two opposing and interdigitating triangular flaps, like when you intertwine your fingers. The midline flap is rotated downward in order to lower the lip line to the normal level. The outward flap is advanced toward the midline to meet it and obliterate the defect. A major advantage of the rotation-advancement repair is that scars are along the natural anatomical features of the upper lip, giving the best esthetic result."

He fell silent as they worked on closing the reformed lip. She'd seen the technique a dozen times before, done it herself twice. But he added an extra function to it, modifying it in subtle touches that made sure the lip was longer, the muscles relaxed so there wouldn't be contracture or scarring later. Usually, after the primary function-correcting procedure, esthetic revision surgery followed after the scar had totally settled to make the lip line even and the face more symmetrical. But she had no doubt that when Vidal was through, little Omar wouldn't need any further surgery.

With the last suture she cut for him she again felt those exhausted vibes emanating from him. If was as if he'd been holding them in, drawing on his stamina reserves, his very lifeforce, to get the job done. Now that it was, he was slipping again.

Apprehension slithered down her nerves. The moment he declared the surgery a wrap and the video camera was turned off while preparations for the second procedure was underway, she turned to him.

"Vidal?"

He knew what she was going to say and chose to divert her. "So you weren't kidding when you said maxillofacial surgery was a special interest. Great to know. Tomorrow you get to pick all the cases you want to do yourself. Also pick your assistants. Not that guy Khaled something or other, though. He's liable to cause some serious harm, staring at you."

He'd noticed that? And was what—jealous? Ha, sure. He'd have to care first, and he didn't—about anything. Her nearness didn't affect *his* performance, that was for sure. Which was as it should be, of course. Fully commendable on the professional, reasonable level. Infuriating and demoralizing on the unreasoning, primitive, feminine one. To know that he could shut her out so completely when his effect on her was unremitting. Not to mention exponential.

She followed him to scrub for the next operation. They finished quickly and before he turned to go back to the surgical stations, he looked over his shoulder. "Ready for a few more rounds?"

His voice—that harsh-velvet rumble! *Don't you dare shudder.*

She turned to him, noticed the renewed vigor in his stance. So, he'd recharged somehow. And there she was, stupidly worrying over him. "Sure. And ready for more hands-on time, since you so graciously admitted I wasn't exaggerating my abilities."

His eyebrows rose. "I wasn't about to take your word for it. The dear lessons of experience...and history, you understand?"

"What's that supposed to mean?"

"Just that my memory serves me well, remembering the girl whose books looked as good as new the night of her final exams. Who considered studying to be the most refined form of torture. Who had her father transferring her around a dozen schools after she'd flunked as many times."

"Gee, I wonder how that girl made it through med school in the top five per cent of her class, then bagged one of the most grueling surgical residency programs in the country."

"How, indeed? I'm still trying to figure it out. I have to admit I thought you went through all that with a few helping hands up from entranced professors..."

"Speaking from experience here, too? Though in your case I'd say you made it all the way up with entranced *clients'* help!"

He didn't even try to make a comeback or a denial, just twisted his lips in that sarcastic in-your-face gesture that told her he couldn't care less what she thought. He went on as if she hadn't interrupted him. "But after seeing you in action, I have to admit that no amount of besotted males could have supplied you with that level of efficiency and knowledge. Even if they'd offered their all, you had to have been extremely eager and capable of learning. Which is the real surprise here. When and how did the reform occur? Was there a man involved?"

Yes, you! she almost blurted out. *You. It always came down to you!*

Her father, though he loved her and her sister and brother completely, had been proudest of Vidal. Her sister and brother had taken it in their stride, secure in their father's love, content with their place in his heart, in his esteem. But not her. From day one, being the youngest, she'd been possessive, about both Vidal and her father. She'd wanted to be the center of attention of both of them. She'd failed with Vidal. Vidal had only had attention for himself. And she hadn't been able to compete with him for her father's esteem. So she'd got her father's attention another way: the negative way.

After Vidal had gone out of their lives, she'd felt the toll it had taken on her father. The void all that pride and satisfaction he'd had in Vidal's achievements had left behind. She'd done everything she could to fill that void, to replace him as her father's object of pride. And though her own achievements had started out that way, she'd continued because it was how she'd become. How she'd been all along, she suspected. Vidal's presence in her life so early on, his intense effect on her, had only thrown her off track.

And he dared taunt her about it? Dared say 'reform'?

Squaring her shoulders, she threw him her most annihilating, disdainful glance. "I'm not the one who had to reform, Vidal. In the end I was just a stupid teenager, going through a phase filled with stupid hair color experiments and other such nonsense. *I* didn't set up scams or con people out of thousands of dollars by the time I was ten, or have a very successful house-burgling and antique resale career by the time I was thirteen. At my worst, I never pointed a loaded gun in a man's face, and I'm certainly not the one boasting both a sentence and time in prison."

CHAPTER FIVE

"My God, but you're cruel!"

Ashley's face was twitching. Any moment now she'd burst out laughing. It was just what Cassandra needed.

"You just *pulverized* the man." Ashley was starting to splutter now, trying to hide it by pretending to smooth her thick brown hair until the man in question was safely out of sight and earshot.

Cassandra rolled her eyes. "Oh, for heaven's sake. I only told him the truth."

Ashley's brown eyes filled. "Told you you were cruel. Don't you know the truth is the ultimate weapon of mass destruction? You want to hurt a man, you tell him the truth."

"Khaled *is* young enough to be my son and he just had to face it."

"He's just a few years younger, four, five at most."

"Which, to me, makes him young enough to be my son!"

"You like older men, huh?"

"*Men*, period. I don't think the male of our species deserves the name before thirty. Forty even. Sometimes never!"

"Or maybe you just like a certain older man?"

Oh, here it comes.

She had to give Ashley credit, though. She'd lasted six full days before bringing it out in the open.

Six full days of escalating torture! Being with Vidal almost every waking moment, spending her nights listening to his every move through her cardboard wall at the hotel Fadel had never transferred them from.

The last thing she needed to crown her perpetual agitation was the intern, Khaled Bou H'maida, chasing after her with invitations and hopes for the future, his eyes glued to her red hair and creamy complexion.

She had been surprised at first as Casablanca was full of foreigners and redheads were by no means a rarity. Then she'd learned he came from Fez, one of the older and far less cosmopolitan cities of Morocco, where segregation of the sexes was the rule and foreign presence was scarce. It had all made sense then. Not the part where he hadn't been able to take a polite no for an answer, though.

She disliked the guy for pushing her into an unpleasant confrontation to drive him away once and for all. Disliked him more for ruining her first leave from the Jet and probably her last. Before she'd turned on him, she'd been really enjoying the walk down one of Casablanca's few traditional markets, among the piled carpets, pottery, jewelry, brassware, and woodwork, finally getting a taste of Morocco's rich heritage.

"Boy, you're more than cruel!" Ashley exclaimed. "You're going to leave me stewing in my curiosity, aren't you?"

"This is about that time at the airport, isn't it?"

"Hel-lo? What else? I wouldn't have been curious at all if that scorching scene hadn't been followed by a subzero chill. On both your parts. What's the deal?"

Cassandra stopped, pretending to inspect a bag of *maronquinerie*, the highly prized local leatherware as she regrouped. *Go for concise and mostly true.* "No deal. We go way back. My father is Vidal's foster-father. We always had a cat-and-dog thing going." She almost winced at the inaccuracy of the simile. If she'd been the dog, he certainly hadn't been the cat. He hadn't run away, only to sit just out of her reach, thoughtful, disdainful, waiting for a chance to retaliate. He'd run away. Period.

"Hard to picture *him* in dog mode!" Ashley chuckled. So even a total stranger knew Vidal would never pursue anyone. "Though, come to think of it, the man *was* all over you in that VIP lounge. That's where it gets tangled, the sizzling-

freezing blasts I keep getting from both of you. Did you use to have an intimate thing?"

"No!"

Oh, what the heck. Just tell her. She already thought worse.

Minutes later, Ashley's explosive fit of laughter brought the whole busy market to a standstill.

"Share the joke?"

She jumped. Ashley did, too.

Vidal! He'd materialized right behind them.

"You—you just about gave me a heart attack, Vidal," Ashley choked. "Where did you come from?"

"From the Jet. Where else?"

"You beamed directly from there?" Cassandra spat, struggling not to sound or look as rattled as she really was.

"A whole army could have marched up to you and you wouldn't have noticed. I haven't seen anyone laughing so hard since Cassandra's debut as the magic mirror in her kindergarten's *Snow White* play."

"*I* wasn't laughing. And neither were you that day." No, he certainly hadn't laughed. He'd sat there, silent, sullen, a sixteen-year-old giant among her family and classmates' families, a mysterious and dangerous creature among the domesticated people who'd populated her life. Had it been any wonder he'd fascinated her so much?

So what was her excuse now?

The same, it seemed. And more. Far more, now she saw dimensions to him she'd never suspected...

His resonant drawl shattered her musings. "No, you weren't laughing. A master prankster never does. So, what's your latest?"

Ashley must have felt the electric storm building. She fidgeted. "Uh, guys, I see this jewelry box over there that I just have to haggle for. Meet you at the square in half an hour when Fadel comes to pick us up?"

Vidal inclined his head in gracious agreement and Ashley almost staggered away.

What he did to women. Without even trying. Damn him.

"So, what was it the whole of Casablanca screeched to a halt to watch? Let me laugh with you."

"Oh, you laugh?"

"On rare occasions. That's why I could use a good laugh now."

"If you're sure you're good at laughing at yourself."

Lazy slits of bright silver mocked her, and the busy market disappeared. "I'm good at a lot of things."

The warm Moroccan sunset threw golden shadows on his dominant bones, struck silver sparks off raven hair, bronze glints off teak skin. Skin that was no longer opaque with depletion, glowing with the return of vigor—of passion. Oh, why did he have to be so beautiful? So mesmerizing?

But…had that been a suggestive remark? From any other man, it certainly would have been. From Vidal, too, if she hadn't been who she was.

He looked away, releasing her, huffed something under his breath. "Laughing at myself is certainly one of them." If it had been a suggestive remark, he'd clearly decided it was a horrible idea. "Let's walk."

He clasped her elbow and she swayed into him. His arm went around her, instinctive, steadying—burning.

Push away, don't let him do this to you, make you join the ranks of mindless, clinging limpets.

He pushed away first. This was getting humiliating.

"You haven't bought anything. Too busy turning local men's heads?"

When it was women, of all ages and nationalities, gawking at him? "I could say the same for you!"

"*I'm* turning local men's heads?"

She pulled her most ridiculous face at him. His sculpted lips parted, tilted up, revealing a glimpse of teeth, perfect but for those too sharp canines. Then there it was. The full heart-stopping sight. And her heart obeyed, stopped, wouldn't start again.

He was smiling at her. He shouldn't be smiling at her. He *didn't* smile.

"Come on, I want to show you something." He towed her after him, her hand engulfed in his, melting, helpless—safe.

This was too confusing. She shouldn't be feeling these overriding emotions for him. Out of the multitudes of men she'd ever met, why him? The systematic paragon of efficiency, the self-acknowledged emotional void?

Whatever horrible experiences he'd had, growing up, they'd shaped him. Her family's love and caring hadn't changed a thing in him. Hadn't cured a thing. It only proved he was incurable. While she'd had the most stable life, the most adjusted psyche, all her blips harmless, and all because of him.

Did she have a death wish, approaching, even looking into the void?

It had to be the proximity, a severe case of opposites attracting.

If only it was just attraction! Physical, unbridled, reason-annihilating. If only it stopped with her wanting to rip his clothes off, rub herself all over him, fill her senses to bursting with him, all of him. All that, what she'd never even imagined feeling, would have been bad enough. But there was more. And more every day.

Six days. Each crammed with a lifetime's worth of starkly revealing experiences, each one tearing away more of her prejudices. Vidal wasn't the man she'd thought he was. The potent force for good with his humbling efficiency, his effortless leadership, his remarkable aptitude with patients. All this couldn't be an act—wasn't one.

What was worse, the 'opposites attracting' theory didn't hold water either. The electricity between them was constantly crackling because they were too much alike, had too much in common. History, tastes, attitudes, approach to life—unbearable attraction. Or was that just her fevered perception?

Even if not, what did all that matter? He was off limits. By choice. His.

He stopped in front of a stall so suddenly she bumped into him. "There it is."

He turned to her with that soul-wrenching smile and her insides quivered. This was getting worse by the second.

She had to squint to focus on what he was pointing at—a huge silver-plated tray with the most intricate, genie-lamp-like teapot and a set of exquisite hand-painted glasses.

"That *is* what you asked Fadel about yesterday?"

She stared at the teaset, dumb, numb. Her synapses were fried. *Say yes.* She only wanted to ask him when he'd heard her, how come he'd remembered.

Stop it. Don't go looking for signs of caring where there are none.

She struggled to answer, to make sense. "Yes. Yes—Mom is crazy about collecting teasets."

He nodded, his smile disappearing. "I know." He turned to the Berber salesman and in seconds had him wrapping it up.

She clung to his arm. "I'm paying for this."

"No."

Just no?

Memories of that time in the airport when he'd said that, just like that, flooded her. Infuriating. Masterful. *Delicious.*

And he'd just bought her a present!

Well, bought her mom a present, but… Hmm, what would he do if it *was* for her?

She raised one eyebrow, recovering, her imp back in residence. "My, aren't we in a generous mood?"

"It's just a hundred and fifty dollars."

"You didn't even haggle."

"Life's too short."

"And since it is, one should take advantage of such opportunities." She shot him her brightest smile, her gaze darting from the next stall back to his eyes, full of meaning. His shutters went down with a slam.

That reaction was not what she'd had in mind. Which was a good thing, since what she'd had in mind was crazy!

When he talked, he sounded just the same. "See anything that you like?"

You! Instead, she sighed, "The whole stall?"

He didn't even bat an eyelid, got out his credit card. "We'll have to ship it home, though. No place on the Jet."

The man was serious!

But not as serious as what was happening to her.

Vidal turned to the salesman, saw him almost salivating at the sight of his credit card.

His heart was booming so loudly he could barely hear his own voice, barely stand. Cassandra was teasing him again. Delighting him again. Addicting him.

He shouldn't have come after her. There had been a million things to do during the four-hour break. Sweeping the Jet, for instance.

He should have known she'd handle Khaled. He *had* known. He didn't have to come after her like a jealous puppy. Jealous? Of Khaled? At all?

He *had* gone over the edge. This total breakdown of control and judgement had to be a terminal symptom of his depression. But...

But he no longer felt depressed.

Apprehensive, agitated, provoked, eager, idiotic, perpetually aroused—you name it. But no longer down, no longer feeling locked in a claustrophobic, pitch-dark cell and wishing to remain there forever. He felt...felt...

"Still sick?" Cassandra's voice filtered into his chaos, filled with that concern that tore at him with a rending desire for it to be real, personal.

"No, I'm not."

"For a moment there..."

"I'm fine. So where do you want your things sent? To your family's or do you have your own place?"

"I have my own place, but—"

He got out a pen and a card from his jacket's inner pocket. "Just write it down here. I'll take care of it."

"Someone needs to take care of *you*, if you go around spending money like that! C'mon Vidal, enough now."

"You don't like the things?"

"What's not to like? They're all gorgeous. But you know I was kidding."

"I'm not."

She sighed, her smile as broad as ever. His guts made a violent attempt to strangle each other. "Strangely enough, I believe you. Though you are *un*believable. Do you go around buying women whole shops?"

"No. And this is not a shop and you're not..." He stopped, caught back "not just *a* woman, you're *the*..." just in time.

"Not a woman!" She completed a far safer version. "In your opinion I belong to a species of imp."

"Even those have addresses. Write yours down."

"Thanks, but no. Really. It's the thought that counts and all that."

"You do realize if we walk away now, without buying something substantial, that man is going to have a stroke? Now, be a good imp and pick something."

She laughed, a melodic sound of pure beauty. Pure torment. It must have shown on his face, for that concern flared again in her eyes.

"Oh, OK, I'll take that, that—and that, and let's get you off your feet. You really don't look so hot."

Strange. He was burning up.

That, that and that turned out to be a belt made of dangling, sparkling beads, a headdress made of the same materials—and a belly-dancing costume. All the color of her eyes.

She *was* out to reduce him to ashes.

In a couple of minutes she was walking beside him, huffing, having almost had to hit him to wrench her things from him. "I've really had it with your macho-ness! This stuff is heavy and whatever you're suffering from, that big secret you don't talk about, you're not recovered from it yet."

Oh, he'd recovered. What he was suffering from now had no cure.

They sat down in a typical Moroccan café, ordered the national beverage—mint tea—and waited for Ashley, Dick and Louisa to converge for Fadel's pick-up time.

She went straight for the jugular. "Have you had tests done? Or are you being the strong big doctor who knows it all and needs none of it?"

Just as well to tell her, get it over with.

"Eight months ago I was in Tibet." Her eyes widened, but she didn't interrupt. "A colleague of mine, Dave Cole, went mountain climbing and didn't return. I organized a search party, we found him, then on the way down a blizzard hit us. By the time we managed to make it down, we were all suffering from severe exposure and hypothermia. One of my guides even had frostbite, had to have two fingers amputated. The eight of us developed pneumonia. After two months most were on the road to recovery but I lagged behind. But I was on my feet so I resumed my normal schedule. And had one relapse after another. Dave, who's a clinical pathologist, made me have comprehensive tests. He thought my inability to get back to normal was a sign of something serious, something that was messing with my immune system."

And Dave had been right.

Cassandra didn't even try to fight the black wave. She wanted to faint. Anything but hear what he had to say.

Was he going to tell her he had AIDS?

"I let him poke and probe me for all he was worth. He found hemoglobin low, white blood cells high, but nothing to be alarmed at."

"Did—did you have…" She gulped, unable to say it.

"AIDS tests? They were the first thing he did. I told him it wasn't a possibility but he had to find out for himself."

He didn't have it. He didn't. Oh, thank you, God *thank you*.

Suddenly she wanted to hit him, break that warrior nose

of his. He must have known what she'd think! Had he meant to scare her to death?

And how would he know it would hit you that hard? When you've made him think you don't care at all?

Oblivious to her state, he stirred his tea and went on. "I stopped all treatments two months ago, became resigned I had my resistant strains for life."

"Did you even think you should just *rest*? Let your body's natural resistance have a chance to fully cure you?"

"I don't need to rest."

"Do you know how annoying you are?"

Vidal raised his eyes, found a fully fledged storm brewing in eyes turned turbulent azure. Just in time to avoid the storm breaking over him, their colleagues joined them, drowned them in conversation, showing off souvenirs. Then Fadel came and they were on their way to the hospital they were performing their evening surgery list in.

Cassandra glared at him all the way, her parting glance at the women's changing room an aggravated bolt.

He entered the men's room, sagged on a bench, closed his throbbing eyes.

He had an idea why she was so angry. In the lifetime of the last six days, he'd come to know her. The new Cassandra. Still fiery, appallingly potent, but rock-solid, responsible, exceptional in everything, from people and patient skills to surgical talents. She hated nonsense, wanted everything logical and to the point, no loose ends, no loopholes. His not taking time off must strike her as stupid, illogical. Unacceptable. She didn't suffer fools gladly.

He suffered—period. With wanting her. He'd never known he had it in him, to want so violently, so uncontrollably. To forget everything else, to fantasize for snatches of time, mindless moments, about things he'd never thought to have. Things he'd never have since he had nothing to give in return.

He had nothing to offer. Nothing he had to offer was worth having.

He would always be alone.

That was why he hadn't gotten better. There'd been no point.

But he *was* better now. He hadn't coughed once in three days. Was that what being near Cassandra did? Energized him, restored him?

What then?

He rose, whisked his sweatshirt over his head, reached for scrubs.

Nothing. That was what then.

"Vidal—the Moroccan minister of the interior wants you," Harry panted.

It was the last day of their two-week stay in Morocco. Their time here had been so smooth, they'd begun to worry when their luck would run out. Now, as Harry appeared at the entrance of the surgical stations, hurried, worried, everyone snapped their heads up, glances flitting from him to Vidal, instantly infected with his anxiety.

Vidal only nodded. "He can wait while I close up."

"Can't someone else do it? He made it sound like the world would end if I didn't produce you out of thin air. He said he was sending people for you."

Vidal frowned. Cassandra's hair stood on end. What was it? What did they want with him?

He stood up. "Cassandra, after you wrap up your case, close up for me. Half-buried vertical mattress sutures all the way. No drains."

She nodded, watched him coming closer. He leaned down, put his mouth to her ear, whispered, "Don't worry, I didn't steal anything."

His words hit her as hard as his warm breath, his overwhelming scent. Heat rushed to her head, purple blanked her vision. She deserved that one. She hadn't even apologized for throwing his past in his face the other day.

He disappeared after Harry and the compartment buzzed with speculation.

Unable to bear it, she put an end to it. "We'll find out soon enough, people. Back to work."

But they didn't find out. For the next twenty minutes, no news came through the info chain of the Jet's non-surgical personnel and Cassandra felt she was slowly losing her grip. Literally. Her hand trembled as she put the last suture in Vidal's patient. Then she staggered up and to the washroom.

What if it was something serious? An accident? Something had happened to someone dear to him? *Did* he have someone dear to him?

Red-hot jealousy kicked inside her, making her sag against the bulkhead. What was wrong with her? The man was entitled to have loved ones!

No, he wasn't! an outraged voice inside her retorted. How dared he have loved ones, when he didn't care about her family—*her father*? He hadn't even mentioned her father in all the previous two weeks and she hated it, hated him for it, and…and…

Her heart twisted, wrenched. What if this *was* about her father?

She burst out of the washroom and heard helicopters approaching the Jet. She pushed through surprised colleagues, tore through the Jet, found Vidal about to leave it.

"Vidal!"

His head swung round, his surprise at her frantic call, at her pouncing on him and clamping him by the arms, instantly subdued. "—told you not to worry. They just discovered I've swiped the hotel towels. Not serious, just a quick rap on the knuckles."

If he was joking, nothing was wrong…

She punched him on the arm. He smiled, dragged her with him outside.

She gaped. "What's all that?"

There were two army helicopters landing just meters from the Jet and about a dozen vehicles, police cars and black diplomatic limousines approaching it.

"My escorts, I guess. Wonder if I'll ever be heard from again."

"Vidal, stop it. What's going on?"

"They've discovered I'm a terrorist and they're going to extradite me."

"Vidal!"

"Don't set the Jet on fire. My surgical services are needed. Double traumatic amputation during a swordfight."

"But why all the army, police and secret service, men in black stuff?"

"It's the son of some high-powered international tycoon and a member of the royal family."

"You mean there are two casualties?"

"It takes two to swordfight, last I heard."

She poked him hard in the ribs. "Why weren't they brought here?"

"Security and publicity issues, of course."

"Why contact *us*?"

"Sorry to step on your professional ego, Cassandra, but they contacted *me*."

"Hello! Trauma surgeon here? Versed in multidisciplinary surgery techniques? Vital part of the replantation surgical team? Ring any bells?"

"Chimes. But they didn't know that, did they?"

"You know!"

"Oh, yeah. And you're coming with me. You, Joseph, Michael, Louisa and every piece of microsurgical equipment."

"You're going to take the surgical microscope? Don't they have their own in whatever ultra-equipped hospital the country's bigwigs go to?"

"Ever since I had laser surgery to get rid of my glasses I spend hours calibrating every surgical microscope to my personal preferences. I won't have that luxury with theirs. And— Here they come." Half a dozen men, each clearly representing some authority in Morocco, were running up the

Jet's stairs. Before they reached them, Vidal turned to her and said, "Gather the gang, *querida*."

Cassandra had never seen anything like it.

But she bet Vidal saw places like Al Ro'waad Medical Center all the time. Opulent, lavishly equipped, this place was a far cry from all the hospitals and medical centers they'd been to in Morocco so far—from anywhere else she'd ever been. This place was from the future.

Vidal's voice cut through her musing. "Here are our amputated parts. Open the container up, Louisa. Let's take a look."

Cassandra glared at him. Vidal had ordered the amputated parts to be brought into the OR first. That was how she preferred it, too. But did he have to sound so nonchalant about it? She was used to all sorts of gory injuries, but the sight of a severed finger still made her stomach quiver.

The amputated parts were preserved to the letter of tissue deterioration prevention protocols—wrapped in bandages, sealed in a plastic bag, placed in a cooler which was inside a second container filled with ice.

A thumb. And half an arm.

Joseph shook his head. "That must have been some heavy, sharp sword."

"And a sharper temper on the thumb guy. No eye for an eye with him." Michael Albrecci, the orthopedic surgeon, whistled.

Vidal inspected the amputated parts. "Mmm, looks real good."

"What?" Cassandra couldn't believe the man.

Eyes of steel rose to her. "Clean amputation, guillotine type. The best for replantation. You have another opinion?"

Put that way, no. She just had issues with his sangfroid. Which was no issue now. On to business. "I'll prep the parts," she said. "You prep the patients."

Vidal nodded and ordered the patients to be brought into

the OR. Joseph walked in with them and reported to Vidal, "Both stable, warm, and sedated."

"Good, let's do this."

Time was of the essence as tissue death was complete in twenty-four hours even in cold storage, and ten hours had already passed. Both teams started their preparations for the replantation operations, preparing both sides of the severed extremities for reconnection. Both parts and stumps had to be meticulously cleaned then dissected to ensure that replantation was an option. Then the nerves, vessels, muscle and tendons were identified and tagged. It was over an hour before both teams finished. Then it was the bones' turn.

Vidal turned to Michael. "What do you think? Bones need to be shortened?"

Michael seemed to consider the options. Bones sometimes needed to be shortened for the reconnection to be done without tension, which would mean subsequent tissue death and failure of replantation. "Nah, tissue loss is negligible. You'll be able to reconnect all structures and close the skin without tension. I'll just fix them."

"Do that."

Half an hour later Michael had fixed the bones with screws and wires to secure them in their original positions and Vidal said, "Arm patient first, then."

"I'll go for both general and regional anesthesia on him," Joseph said. "To enhance blood flow in the injured limb."

Vidal nodded approval. "Good idea. Gather round, team. This is going to be interesting."

It was. Cassandra had never taken part in a replantation surgery involving such a major limb part.

She got to go first, repairing the muscles and tendons. It took over an hour to repair them, first the extensor muscles, those that stretched the arm, then the flexors, those that contracted it. Then it was Vidal's turn and the really tricky part, repairing both vessels and nerves.

As he took her place at the surgical microscope, she didn't envy him his task. He'd be working on nerves and vessels that were down to a millimeter or less in diameter, and he had to restore them to their proper function.

"Not repairing veins first?" Cassandra asked when he picked an artery end with his forceps.

"No."

Just no. After two weeks of a constant diet of 'just nos,' she should be used to it. Without another word, he went on to reconnect every artery in the mid-arm, pausing frequently for her to irrigate the lumen with diluted heparin solution to avoid clot formation. After he was finished, he turned his attention to the veins. Like everyone else, Cassandra was holding her breath, entranced by his unbelievably delicate and precise actions, the total silence making her blood thump in her ears.

When he was finished with the veins, Vidal suddenly spoke. "If veins are anastomosed first, the carbon dioxide and all other metabolic debris in the blood they carry only accelerate muscle degeneration. And as you saw, establishing arterial inflow first made the veins' identification easier when they filled with blood."

Made sense. Worked, too. Although it went against common practice, his method did work better.

After another indeterminate stretch of time, he'd reconnected the nerves, then moved his head away from the microscope. "And now, ladies and gentlemen, skin coverage and then it's on to the thumb."

All in all, they spent nine hours in OR.

Considering they'd been at the end of their day at the Jet, their last, crazy, crammed-with-last-minute-things day in Morocco, they were way past dead on their feet.

But it wasn't meant to be that they would rest.

The moment they staggered out of OR, the crowd of officials who'd escorted them to the facility pounced on them. After endless questions about the operations and their expected outcomes, they dragged Vidal away to see the relatives of the two young men.

For half an hour, the team waited for him in the most incredible waiting room Cassandra had ever seen, with its floor to ceiling windows overlooking the snowcapped Atlas mountains.

Then he returned, leaned on the door and sighed. "Our patients' parents are fighting over who will host us in their palaces tonight. What do you say?"

"I say we go to arm guy's palace. He was a lot more work." Michael chuckled.

Louisa poked him. "You're gross, Michael."

Vidal rubbed his eyes and neck. "Play nicely, children. Now, pick."

"Why can't we go back to our hotels?" Cassandra asked.

"Because we're being more or less abducted in gratitude. I was just too tired to resist. All I want is a bed right now."

That was all Cassandra wanted, too. A bed with Vidal in it.

What was she thinking?

Exactly what you want, an internal voice sighed.

Joseph stood up, clapped his hands and headed for the door. "If they won't release us, let's save ourselves the hassle and split up, satisfy both parties."

Michael followed him. "Yeah, you and Cassandra go with the arm guy's people. That way, when he wakes up and decides we've botched his operation, *we'll* be safe with his enemy's people."

Louisa poked him, harder this time. "You really *are* gross, Michael!"

Vidal huffed an exhausted, derisive sigh as they walked out of the hospital. "So we're your scapegoats, huh?"

Michael nodded. "You're the one who says the leader has to take the worst. Take it, baby."

Vidal shrugged. "I guess I will. Just to see this day end. Will you, Cassandra?"

"I don't know why I should!" she bristled as they reached the limousines awaiting them. "This high-handed treatment, whisking us away from our jobs, keeping us here whether we like it or not—''

''Oh, I like it!'' Michael chipped in.

Joseph pushed him into the car. ''Stuff it, Michael. Your good mood is starting to grate. See you tomorrow, guys.''

Minutes later, Vidal was sprawled out beside her in the back seat of the limousine, his eyes closed all the way to their destination. She sat rigidly, aware of him in every cell, fighting. Just before she lost the fight and snuggled up to him, they stopped.

A guard held the vehicle door open for her and she got out to the sight of a palace out of the Arabian Nights—just a lot more extravagant. The sheer magnificence and artistry of every detail on the way in stunned her, taking her mind off the man walking just a footstep behind her and all the wild feelings he provoked. Her trance lasted until she heard Vidal saying *Shokrun*—thanks in Arabic—to the escort who showed them into the most amazing apartment and left.

Were they supposed to share it?

Well, why not? It was huge. Surrounding the huge reception area, she counted eight closed doors, each opening into a room, even a suite, no doubt. Each of them would have total privacy.

Still, it *was* an apartment and to assume they'd share it… Oh, it was only for tonight. And she knew Vidal would never try anything.

Even if she wanted him to?

Sleep. Just go to sleep and stop being crazy.

She opened one door, entered, gaped. Among flickering oil lamps, swirling incense fumes and gossamer falls of drapes from the ceiling was a nine-foot circular bed draped in deep red satin…

''They'll bring food and clothes.'' Vidal's voice came from the doorway. She whirled around, uncoordinated, quaking. ''I won't bother waiting for either.''

Just before he walked on, she exclaimed, ''You're OK with this, aren't you? It doesn't bother you that we left our humanitarian mission to come and tend two spoilt brutes who play with lethal weapons? Who'll probably do it again?''

"We're doctors, Cassandra. We don't question if our patients deserve our help or not. Are you a reverse snob? They don't deserve our help because they're rich?''

"They could have gotten anyone they wanted from anywhere in the world in time. They didn't have to snatch us from the people who don't have alternatives.''

"It was a simple matter of triage. The amputated parts were becoming nonviable by the second and we had the best team in reach who could do the job, in the *best* time. Surely that takes priority over the elective surgeries we were involved in?''

Suspicion hit her, congealed into conviction. "They're paying you, aren't they?''

"Of course they are. Obscenely. They can afford it.''

"You—you…'' Accusations balled in her throat, choking her.

"I'm what, Cassandra? Mercenary? Despicable? Cold-blooded? Self-serving?'' A step closer, crowding her backwards, accompanied each word. "I've heard all that before.''

He had? Who had told him? Her father?

"And you know what? I've had enough.''

Her knees hit the edge of the bed. She tumbled onto it, the bouncing mattress jerking her up, making her lose all coordination. Then she lay there, staring up at him, losing all reason.

He bent over her, a knee on either side of her, hands going to hers, spreading her arms and holding them down, his eyes ominous stormclouds, the hard planes of his face shifting with indecipherable emotions. Then he finally rasped, "*Enough*, Cassandra.''

And he moved. Away. Leaving her. No!

She caught him back, brought him on top of her, hard, heavy, full, moaned denial and hunger into his flesh.

"No—not enough!''

CHAPTER SIX

SHE'D been waiting all her life. Yearning. For this. For Vidal.

And she'd never even realized. Never admitted it. Pure self-preservation, that. For what would she have done about it if she had? He'd always been out of reach, in every sense.

Now he was here, in her arms, and it was too much—the relief almost agony. Vidal, close at last. Covering her, imprinting her, their breaths, their heartbeats mingling. She wanted more, wanted everything. Wanted to open up to him, lay bare all that she was, share every freedom, surrender every secret. Now.

Vidal. Cassandra savored his weight on top of her, his power, the masculinity that formed every bone and muscle, the virility in which her lips were buried at the opening of his shirt. Liquid desire burned its way inside her, the pangs of hungry pleasure becoming pain.

Oh, why wasn't he moving? Doing something? Didn't he want this?

No—no, he did. His desire was blatant, daunting even, digging into her stomach through their clothes, his breath fracturing, his body shuddering.

But...that could be just an automatic male reaction.

Doubts crashed in on her. He hadn't given one sign that he wanted her, not since he'd found out who she was. Now it was she who'd dragged him, who was holding him now, stopping him from getting up even if he'd wanted to. Did he want to? Was the unbearable longing all on her side?

Oh, God, what would she do then?

Let him go. Let this go. Tell him you didn't mean it, were just too tired, wanted comfort, want to apologize...

No.

She'd come this far. She had him in her arms. It wouldn't do any more harm if she found out for sure whether he wanted to be there or not.

Vidal finally located his voluntary controls, raised his head, stared down at Cassandra.

This couldn't be happening.

She couldn't be there, beneath him, her yielding flesh cushioning his every quivering muscle, her whimpered breathing filling his lungs, her heart beating inside his chest.

He'd been dreaming every night since he'd seen her again. After years of dark oblivion, dreams filled his sleep. Explicit, abandoned, full of color and sound and heat and scents. Hot, mingling bodies, wrestling together for a closer fit. And every morning he'd woken up in pain, cursing the day he'd given in and come on this mission.

But no dream had been this bad, this preposterous, this fabulous. He didn't have it in him to be that inventive. Even the setting was over the top. Red satin, gossamer drapes, shimmering oil lamps and amber and musk incense. And what she'd done!

In his dreams he'd always reached for her, captured her even, forced her to stop pushing him away long enough to arouse her, persuade her to give in to the passion he knew they could share. Now it was she who'd captured him. That, above anything else, should confirm that it was all in his mind.

But it wasn't. It was real. She'd made the first move.

Now what? *Dios*, now what?

Take her. Rip her out of her clothes, worship her, pleasure her, then take her. Brand her. Do it now before she changes her mind.

No. No way. Nothing had changed. Or ever would. And, anyway, she didn't want him. She just wanted sex.

So give it to her. Maybe then she'll start wanting you.

And what if she didn't? What if she couldn't?

Then at least you would have had her for a while.

A while? For the rest of this mission? Less? Of course it would be for less. And afterwards? How could he live with what he'd done? He didn't need to add more crimes to his record. If he got up and left now, at least he'd never face himself with his reality. He could go on ignoring it, living with it.

Living? You call this empty existence living?

No, but it was all he had, all he could ever have. Now he had to tear himself away…

"Vidal." Her arms went around him, her hands pressing into his back, her voice into his mind, her hunger into his body.

No use. No use struggling.

Eternal damnation would be a small price for anything with her.

Vidal moved, away again. Something hot and agonizing cascaded inside Cassandra's chest. Had her heart burst open?

She'd just had to find out for sure, hadn't she? Repeat past mistakes when she should have known better now. Should have grown up. Given up.

But he wasn't leaving her this time, just gliding down to even out their positions, rubbing against her, bearing down now, his knee carving a space between her thighs.

"Cassandra, *querida*…?" He rose above her, not distant now, hard-hitting, clear, raw. Wanting her. *Her.* No doubt about it.

That was all she needed or would ever need.

She arched, answering his unvoiced question, demanding his all. He obeyed, gave her what she was quaking for, thrust at her empty ache, offering comfort, aggravating the gnawing. Her shudders intensified, her legs closed around him, suffocating for his breath, starving for his taste.

She dragged his head down, caught his lips, cried out with the poignancy of the long-craved contact. He caught the red-hot admission in his mouth, growled his own, his tongue driving into her, no hesitation now. She returned his voracious kiss, letting him drink deep, drink all. One hand smoothed her hair, convulsed in it, the other melted down her face, her neck, greedy, anxious, paused before venturing any further, asking. Oh, how could he not know her answer?

Give it to him. She had to produce the words around the lump of urgency in her throat. "Vidal—need you—your hands—everywhere!"

Those miraculous hands needed no more than her choking plea. They melted her clothes, then her flesh. Took breasts stinging for his touch, cupped them, smoothed them, kneaded them. Ah, that look of driven voraciousness—Lord, she'd missed it, hadn't felt alive without it.

He slid down her body, one hand against the middle of her back, arching her, thrusting her breasts forward, an offering for his pleasure, the other cupping her buttocks, raising her for his full domination. One breast then the other was suckled, worshipped, devoured. When her cries turned to pleas he came up, drove his tongue inside her, filled her, drank her. "*Te quiero—te quiero*, Cassandra, *ahora…*"

"What…?"

His smile was a grimace, his breathing labored, his every muscle resonating in tune with her own trembling. "You make me forget, language—everything. I said I want you—now—but…" He frowned and her heart clenched. Hesitation. Asking him to explain had broken the spontaneity, was giving him time to think, to withdraw… No!

"Yes, Vidal, yes, now!" She hugged him tighter, arms and legs, buried anxious lips and teeth in his corded neck.

His tension rose with his groans, back arching, giving her the opportunity she needed to sink her hunger in the steel chest she'd bared. He jerked. "Cassandra, *querida…*"

"Yes!"

"*Por Dios*—I don't—you don't…"

"Dr Santiago, are you awake?"

The intrusion detonated their sensual cocoon, splintering nerves strung beyond their limits. He lurched. Away this time, up, on his feet in a second.

A heart attack, Vidal thought as he staggered to the bedroom door. This pain had to be at least that. If it were only just in his chest and arms and back...

It didn't matter now. He could die later. He had to stop that man coming to look for him, finding them here, finding Cassandra this way...

She was already fumbling her clothes on, but the sight of her spread for him, open, feverish, begging, annihilating...

Later. You have a lifetime to drag that memory out and go nuts over it.

He was already at the bedroom door, almost slamming it shut, then opening it just a fraction and peeking out at the intruder.

"What is it?" he rasped.

"Ah, Dr Santiago!" Erfan, the escort he'd forgotten all about, came forward, full of smiles. "It's great you're still awake. I brought you and Dr St James a dinner not to be missed, and every sort of clothing you might need. Inside the palace anyway. I'm afraid we couldn't find any tailored clothes to suit *your* height and size. I have people still looking, but on the off-chance we can't find anything suitable I'm going to have to ask you for your clothes, to be washed and pressed for tomorrow."

"That's very kind of you, Erfan, but there's no need."

"There's every need," Erfan insisted. "You just can't wear them in their current condition in your meeting with His Highness in the morning."

With that it was clear the adamant Erfan would stand out there until he handed them to him.

Just give him the damned clothes and get him out of here. And this time lock the door behind him.

With a sigh, feeling Cassandra's eyes on his every move, digging talons of raw lust in his flesh, he stripped out of his clothes. At least he'd worn underwear. Not that it hid anything.

Once Erfan had left the apartment, Vidal limped out and locked the main door.

Then he stood in the middle of the huge reception area in

his boxer shorts, so aroused it was agony to move. But move to go where? Back to Cassandra? *Dios!*

What was she thinking now? What to do, where to go from here?

One thing he knew. He couldn't take her up on her earlier offer—for safety reasons. Mainly. Anyway, the insanity that had come over her back there in that magical room must have lifted already. And not only because of those safety issues.

She came out of the bedroom and his interrupted heart attack resumed. The memory of her, hair cascading over his arm down to same color satin sheets, lush breasts begging for his hunger, lips swollen with his possession, limbs containing him in abandon, burnt a hole in his brain.

"Vidal…"

"Cassandra…"

He fell silent. Couldn't even say, "You first." Though she was first and foremost in his mind, in his senses, he had to let her end this in the way she saw fit. If she still wanted him, there were other ways…

She took a step forward, stopped, stared at him for a long moment, rapid-fire emotions transfiguring her vivid features. Then she ended it just as he'd expected. She turned, re-entered her room, closed her door.

Left him out in the cold.

Cassandra closed the door and crumpled, frustration and humiliation driving her to the floor, right where Vidal had stood, stripping, only minutes ago. Showing her all her desires made human, all the cravings she'd never quench…

Crazy idiot that she was, she'd thought he'd let the man leave, lock the door and come back into her arms. When he hadn't, she'd actually gone after him. Couldn't take a hint, could she? She had to see for herself the blankness she'd come to dread back in his eyes, the withdrawal, take the slap full in the face.

It stung. Burned. Every breath did.

All through the sleepless night, all through the awkward

breakfast and drive back to the Al Ro'waad Medical Center. And now more as she watched him at the podium of the huge lecture hall, addressing the team of doctors that would follow up the replantation patients. He was magnificent in the black formal suit they'd managed to get for him. Was this frighteningly distant man the same one who'd branded her with his passion only last night?

Force the debilitating memories aside. Focus.

He'd just finished his commentary on both procedures' videos, and was now detailing follow-up. ''Dressing removal in ten days, in the OR under regional block to alleviate pain and prevent vasospasm, which would endanger circulation. An IV bolus of heparin is also indicated. Moving the replanted part to be in no less than a month. In the meantime, skin color, swelling and temperature should be carefully monitored. Any change that suggests the reattached part is in jeopardy requires immediate dressing removal as a first measure.''

He reached for a glass of water, gulped it down in one go. With his grim profile still to the audience, he continued, ''Now specifics. The thumb case. The usual cause of a failed digit replantation is venous congestion. Surgical re-exploration won't be an option here so, in case it develops, consider medical-grade leeches. These can be effective in relieving venous congestion, both by actual sucking of venous blood trapped in the replanted digit and by instilling the anticoagulant hirudin, present in its saliva.

''For the forearm case, re-examine the limb in OR three days from now to evaluate the condition of the involved muscles. If you doubt their viability *at all*, go for further debridement—''

''How about giving us a projection of the outcomes of both replantations?'' That was the head of the plastic surgery department. His feathers were clearly irreparably ruffled, having been passed over for Vidal.

Vidal fell silent for a long moment until Cassandra's hair roots prickled. What would he say? The patients' parents were sitting in the back, those people who'd outlaid so much money to save their sons' limbs.

Vidal finally began, ''The average survival rate of replantations is as high as 94 per cent with satisfactory function in selected cases—''

The same doctor cut him off again. ''We'd appreciate some specific, solid projections. Not some hackneyed statistics.''

Vidal turned to him, his eyes lethal. ''You want me to promise a return to full function within the year, don't you? Maybe you like to give your patients false hope, then later blame any complications or poor results on anything else but your performance? I deal in facts and live up to my 'projections'. And here are both! They *will* have cold intolerance, which could be nasty, but if they treat their replanted parts with great care, it *will* subside in about two years. The cosmetic result *will* be far better than prostheses but it *won't* be nearly as good as new. Recovery of sensation and nerve function *will* be as good as can be expected since both are young, with clean, guillotine-like amputations where best results can be obtained, but it won't feel anything like their normal extremities. Oh, and the best they can expect is fifty to sixty per cent of normal active range of motion.''

He paused again, looked at his audience for the first time. ''Questions?''

The silence that had accompanied his barrage deepened into a breath-holding hush. No one was about to ask him anything now.

''If that's all, my team and I would like to return to the Jet now. Thanks for your...hospitality, and best of luck to our patients. For any consultations, we can always be reached within the hour through GAO Central.''

With that, he strode out of the lecture hall, leaving Cassandra and their team to run after him.

Half an hour later, the helicopter was in the air, and Michael was rubbing his hands together. ''So, how much did they fork over?''

Vidal turned his eyes to him. "Five each."

"Five what?" Cassandra squeaked.

"Five million, of course!" Michael rolled his eyes.

"Good for you, Vidal!" Louisa whooped.

"'Good for you, Vidal'?" Joseph growled in outrage. "Each of us has a few hundred grand's worth of work in this heist. Cassandra a million at least!"

"Great! My share pays for the exhaustible supplies, the fuel and the food!" Louisa preened.

Michael winked at her. "And mine for the toilet disinfectant and paper and barf bags. Do you know how much we use?"

"Were you born gross, Michael?" Louisa pretended to barf herself.

OK. Cassandra was confused now. The guys were actually happy Vidal had milked that much money from their patients' fathers? Why? Were they really getting a cut?

No. No, she no longer believed Vidal was that kind of man—despite all evidence to the contrary. So what explained all that? And what was that they were saying about paying for the supplies? What kind of joke was that?

Twelve hours ago, she would have asked, point-blank. Now everything had changed. She felt so shy, so overwhelmed being near him now...

Vidal's cool words cut into her agitation. "It seems Cassandra thinks we're some sort of gang, splitting the loot."

"With you as our mob boss?" Michael guffawed. "If only. Nah, it's nothing that exciting. That ten million is a 'donation' and it means that beside the fifteen millions Vidal has already dished out, he's gone and covered the whole mission's expenses."

"You could have told me."

It was Cassandra's first chance in two weeks to talk to Vidal, and she wasn't wasting it. They were landing in an hour and she had no time for roundabout talk.

He didn't either. He neither pretended to puzzle over her

out-of-the-blue comment or even open his eyes as he said, "And spoil your fun?"

Irritation simmered. He was taking avoiding her too far. She almost shouted, *Enough already. I get the message!*

She'd gotten the message all right. That night in Morocco had been an attack of temporary madness he clearly wanted to delete from time's records.

But the it-was-probably-for-the-best therapy wasn't working. Not when she'd never felt worse. She'd forever remember Muscat, Oman as the setting of the most frustrating, depressing time of her life. All through their time there, Vidal had managed to split them up so they'd never been in the same five-mile radius. Including their accommodation.

Now they were on their way to Hyderabad, she had him where she wanted him, trapped on the Jet, with nowhere to run from her. Too bad if he was done talking to her. She wasn't done talking to him.

She sat down beside him. "I never had fun thinking badly of you, Vidal."

"Really?" His eyes half opened now, turned to her.

"It's you who always had fun making sure I did." And he had. When he'd told her of his past. When he hadn't told her of his huge role in funding the Jet's mission and the Jet itself—GAO itself, even. "Why?"

Something. A flicker in those unreadable eyes. Then he just shrugged.

So he didn't consider her worth the effort of clarification. No matter. He was getting his apology whether he wanted it or not. Whether he cared or not.

"For what it's worth, and it's clearly not worth a lot, I'm sorry. I hate prejudice and I admit I had a lot of that against you. It doesn't matter how I came by it. I should have known better than to rely on hearsay, even if it came from your own lips. I should have tried to be informed before I formed opinions. I like to think I usually do. In your case I went out of my way to be uninformed. Can you forgive me?"

The flicker was a flare now. Quickly veiled when he turned

his eyes away again. "Don't go turning 180 degrees on me now. I don't fancy being made a saint."

She'd missed him so much. Missed his humor, his eyes on her, his voice, his breath, his—everything. And he was talking to her again. That might be all he'd ever do, but right now she was so starved for him that even that little delighted her. She laughed. "You're no saint, Vidal. But you're a good man. A great man. The world needs more men like you."

His rough bark of laughter jolted her. "You don't do anything by halves, do you? I'm either a monster or an angel. Well, I'm neither, Cassandra. And the world would be in a lot more trouble with more men like me."

"Why do you say that when you know it's not true?" Her heart suddenly lightened, his nearness acting as a stimulant. An inhibition-relaxant. Her hand went to his cheek, failed to find enough flesh to pinch, caressed it instead. "You're fishing for more compliments, aren't you? There's plenty more. Got a few days?"

His eyes swung to her again, fierce, explicit—holding back.

Oh, Vidal! I'm only human. She surged up, put her lips to the chiseled angle she'd been caressing. Breathed in, held it, pressed, breathed out. Then sagged back.

A second, an eternity passed, electricity humming, alive. Then in two fierce movements he shoved the armrest between their seats up and hauled her over him, capturing her lips in midair. She met him more than halfway, sinking in his mouth, her tongue dueling with his, fuller, deeper, with all the pent-up craving of the past two weeks.

"Vidal…" *Oh, my love.* He devoured her moans as they formed, didn't know what she'd left unspoken. But she did, the realization ecstasy. Agony.

She loved him.

When he didn't have any idea how to love.

Vidal shuddered, pleasure rocking him with every glide of his lips along her silken, moist flesh, every plunge into her welcoming warmth. Cassandra's hands in his hair bunched, tugged, taking him deeper, higher. His hands weaved in the vivid hair he now lived to look for, her mark, her herald, holding onto her, coming apart with the enormity of it all.

He was losing his mind. Had already lost it, the moment she'd asked his forgiveness, praised him, kissed him—penetrated him. Long before that, even—since that night in Morocco. But at least he hadn't pounced on her in the past two weeks, devoured her right where anyone could have seen them. He'd been pretending sanity, and the only way to keep up the pretense had been by not coming near her, not letting her near. Her distance, even if it had been his doing, had only destroyed what remained of his mind, his control. Now, the moment she'd sought him out, reached out and touched him, generous, tender, unafraid and unembarrassed, his insanity just manifested.

An anxious tug shifted her, took her fully to him, knees on both his sides, her heat even through their clothes forcing his helpless thrust against her. He framed her face with trembling hands, and her quivering smile, before he dragged her down for more abandon, blasted his soul.

He'd lost far more than his mind. He'd lost his separateness. She'd taken away his autonomy. He'd known isolation, but never loneliness. Now his loneliness for her corroded him, would soon finish him.

His strength was almost all gone. Soon nothing would stop him from losing himself in her.

No! Resist, a feeble voice of reason quavered. *For Arthur. Dios l'ayuda*, he couldn't.

God did help him. Next moment Harry's voice came over the Jet's com system. "Sorry to disturb your slumber, folks. Hyderabad airport is right below. Suzie and Ibrahim are coming to make sure you're all upright and strapped in."

"That's no list, that's a phone book!" Cassandra gaped at Vidal's extended hand. "Is everyone in Hyderabad on our list or what?"

Vidal quirked his eyebrow. ''Those are just ten thousand cases.''

''*Just* ten thousand? And I was so proud of our twenty hundred each in Casablanca and Muscat. Excuse me as I faint,'' she mock-swooned.

Scorching comebacks leapt in his eyes and were subdued.

Oh, hell! This vicious circle was getting too much. After every flare of passion he just clamped up, knocking her back to square one.

What drove her insane was her certainty that he wanted her. Physically, at least. So what held him back? What froze him up?

Was it their history? The image of her as a brat superimposed on her current image every time he had a passion-free moment? Or did he have qualms about starting a temporary liaison with her *because* of their history? She had no illusions. Vidal didn't do permanent. His own admission, his own life were the ultimate testament to that. Few men passed forty without even one semi-serious relationship. But, then, few men boasted about total self-sufficiency and emotional imperviousness as he did.

And it was clear he thought an affair with her was too much trouble for the pleasure. But how could she tell him it wouldn't be like that? That she wouldn't cause trouble, she just wanted to be with him...

Simple. She couldn't. She had no right imposing her feelings on him. Hell, she couldn't believe it! She was turning into one of those clingy, needy, self-deluding females after just a few weeks of being exposed to him!

And she wouldn't. Though loving him was a novel experience, a damaging, demoralizing experience, she still had enough dignity and self-control to take no for an answer. If she gave it a real try, she could blow hot and cold with the best of them. And the best of them had to be him.

She tossed her hair back, cleared her head. ''Oh, well, I guess in a country of over a billion people, ten thousand is just a block's population. Are this morning's train accident casualties among those numbers or have they already been distributed to available medical facilities, and our cases are all 'cold' preselected ones?''

''Kishnar Hospital is among those available medical facilities. Harry arranged for the most serious cases to be brought there. We should make use of our A-list trauma surgeon.''

''Ah, high praise, if only the truth. Still worth a kiss, though.'' Reaching up on tiptoe, she gave him a lingering kiss right on his formidable jaw, felt it clench, withdrew with an impish grin. Not bad for a nonchalant, flirtatious attitude if she said so herself. ''OK, the sooner we start and all that. Are you coming to Kishnar Hospital or are you back to avoiding me?''

For answer he studied his feet with the utmost interest. She looked, too, searching for the extra toe that must have warranted that absorption.

Finally he looked up, at some point on the jet's bulkhead behind her head. ''If you can call kissing you senseless just an hour ago avoiding you.''

''What almost knocked me senseless was how fast you flung me back in my seat afterwards.''

''I didn't fling you back. We were landing, you had to buckle your seat belt. Period. And I'm not avoiding you. Why should I?''

Her laugh rang out. ''The list of reasons would be as thick as this phone book. Heading it are the facts that I make you uncomfortable and you don't know what to do about me.''

Another feet-examining moment. ''You'll make me very uncomfortable and I really won't know what to do if you don't help me sort through the cases and assign cases.''

''*After* dealing with all the emergency operations in Kishnar, you mean?''

''Yes—yes, of course. I've split up four thousand cases among our senior surgeons. The rest is up to us. You get cases 4000 through 7000. Once we've wrapped up the emergency lists, we'll have a steady stream of over seven hundred cases a day.''

"That will leave no room for any sort of follow-up!"

"The doctors in our partnering hospitals will do that. We'll have everything on video, with a few minutes added to the end of each procedure detailing follow-up instructions."

"What if those are ten thousand plastic surgery cases?"

"They aren't. About fifteen per cent are dental cases, twenty-five per cent ophthalmological, the rest assorted surgical and medical conditions. At least, that's what I'm told. Nothing is in order, so we'll have to sort them out. And I'm coming to Kishnar Hospital. There are plenty of facial injuries and trauma reconstruction for me to busy myself with."

With that, Vidal turned and walked out of the Jet.

He desperately needed some fresh air. Some distance. Some arrythmhia-free heartbeats.

Cassandra's relentless assault on his senses was shortening his life. And it shouldn't. She was showing him it was all light and unimportant. It should have made him feel better, knowing that he wouldn't be hurting her if he gave in. It didn't. He would still be betraying Arthur. Then there was the despondency of knowing she viewed him as a sort of holiday romance. Nothing more than holiday sex.

"I would have loved to give you a glimpse of my country, taken you through Hyderabad," Karan Malik, their only Indian and gynecologist said from the back of the bus that was carrying them to Kishnar Hospital. "With ten thousand cases in two weeks, I doubt we'll have time to breathe in between."

Vidal watched Cassandra turn to smile at Karan. "Then make the most of the time before we're immersed in work, Karan. Give us a concentrated guided tour."

Karan chuckled. "Nothing about India *can* be concentrated, Cass. It's a land that sideswipes you with its size, clamor and diversity, and the only thing to expect is the unexpected. It's also a litmus test for anyone who comes here. Some visitors are so appalled they can't wait to get on a plane and get away, while those who enjoy delving into complex cosmologies and thrive on sensual overload find India one of the most intricate and rewarding dramas unfolding on earth.''

Cassandra whistled. ''Wow, that's an evocative portrayal. Wonder if I could sell my country that well to a first-time visitor!''

Karan's slightly Indian-laced British drawl deepened. ''So you're one for sensual overload then, Cass?''

Vidal almost bared his teeth at him. Cass? When had she become *Cass* to Karan? And what was with those flirtatious tones and hungry black eyes? And her—with her noncommittal chuckles and her damned irresistibility!

She had to know her effect. Was she using it, stringing along as many males as there were around, just for the heck of it? Was that what she was doing to *him*—still persisting in her attempts to make a fool of him? If it was, what would she do if he gave in? Turn on him later and laugh her head off? What if he didn't? Would she turn to someone else? The handsome Karan, for instance?

Images mushroomed in his imagination, polluting his soul, crushing down further on his sanity. No. No way. No one else. He wouldn't let it happen. Not while he watched.

And how would he stop it? Did he think it would mutilate him any less, imagining her with other men when she was out of his sight, his reach—his life? That he wouldn't want to kill any man who ever had his hands on her?

The man Vidal was developing violent tendencies towards was continuing. ''I come from Agra originally, but I probably know Hyderabad better since I went to Osmania University here.''

''Ah, Agra, home of the Taj Mahal, isn't it?'' Cassandra sighed. ''Now, that's one place it's almost criminal to come to India and not see.''

''The Taj does overshadow everything else in Agra, in India as a whole, yes. To tourists at least. Hyderabad doesn't have one such overwhelming monument, but there are plenty of other magnificent historical sites. Then there's also all your hearts can desire in the way of exotic souvenirs—pearls, silks, jewelry, carpets. But my biggest recommendation is just being among its people, basking in their warmth and hospitality.''

Joseph groaned. "Stop, Karan, if you don't want us to start resenting the work that will stop us experiencing all that!"

Karan's eyes flashed in mischief. "Poor you. You haven't lived until you have sampled the piping hot *malai-puri*, watched the sun set behind Golconda and the Tombs, smelt the bread or the kebabs turning on the spits in the old city, or listened to the cries of wild peacocks in Brahmananda Reddy Park, and touched the 2,500 million-year-old rocks at Durgam Cheravu.''

The women pretended to swoon and Vidal snarled, only half joking, "I see I'll have to kill you to shut you up, Karan!"

CHAPTER SEVEN

"I HEARD pleas for help!"

Vidal turned at her teasing tones. Cassandra just knew he'd known she was there before she'd spoken but had waited for her to before he turned, his moves deliberate, his eyes smoldering with—what? Whatever, it was better than that chill only he could project.

The spacious OR was pandemonium, teeming with medical personnel, five operations taking place simultaneously. A sixth surgical station, the one Vidal had been facing, was still being prepared.

He moved away from it now, closing the gap between them until he was touching her, whisper touches, his thigh to her hip, his chest to her shoulder, bringing back that first day at Madrid Airport, when he'd been so eager for her, so spontaneous. He leaned down, drawled an inch from her ear, "Not from me, you didn't."

Images of pulling him down, devouring those maddening lips, flashed into her mind. She was still aching from their loss when he'd wrenched them out of her reach back on the Jet. *Do it!*

Oh, help! She was really losing it. Thinking of kissing him in the middle of the busiest OR she'd ever seen. Then again, compared to what she'd done back on the Jet, straddling and devouring him, it wasn't such a big deal.

Get a grip, woman!

She took a step backwards, adjusted her cap. "Weird! So who was it who sent for me as I finished my last laparotomy, telling me to get here immediately?"

He pressed closer again, took her arm, led her to the secluded corner by the scrubbing and gowning area. "I just thought you'd find this case interesting, since maxillofacial surgery is a special interest of yours, and..." He paused when she stifled a yawn and let go of her arm. It tingled, ached with the loss of his touch. "You don't have to stay, though. If you're tired, tell Harry to escort you to the hotel. He handled matters this time, got us a four-star place."

"I've done four abdominal explorations, five thoracotomies, examined thirty other non-surgical cases and, strangely enough, I'm not tired."

His eyes flashed silver when she aborted another yawn. "I've heard that before, from surgeons who fell asleep in mid-incision!"

Maybe she should tell him she was yawning with oxygen deprivation. She hadn't drawn one good breath since he'd summoned her. "I hear you did even more procedures. What makes *you* impervious to fatigue?"

That he was back to normal, and that his 'normal' turned out to be about three hundred per cent of any other mortal's full capacity, still didn't mean that a dozen major operations in as many hours wasn't pushing it too far.

"Don't tell me you haven't heard the rumor that I'm an android?"

Is that why you're so perfect? So...unapproachable? Her heart convulsed with loss and futility.

Keep it light.

She looked him up and down, knew it was a mistake just as she pretended to perform the saucy appraisal. Even the ugly green scrubs couldn't hide his sheer, brutal attraction and virility, didn't lessen his impact on her. *Keep it light!* "Oh, that's what 'paragon of efficiency' means? What powers you, then?"

His eyes swept her in return, told her, *I've seen you out of those shapeless things. I've touched and I've tasted. I remember. And I hunger.* "Right at this moment?"

Oh, my! This was a very clear come-on. She'd sworn she wouldn't pursue him any more, that she'd spare herself the misery. She knew she'd never get over him, that she'd never want another man, never feel anything like this, yet she'd hoped she was sane enough not to turn their time together into a crippling injury. But if he'd changed his mind...

Suddenly he straightened, exhaled. "Go get some sleep, Cassandra. You've done your quota for today."

Oh, Lord. The man was a professional, devastating, merciless *tease!*

He'd sent for her, flirted with her and now he was stepping away again. Well, tough. She was damned if she'd let him. He could step away all he liked on the personal level. He'd brought her here and here was where she'd stay, working with him again.

"I'm staying. Period."

"This is going to be a very long operation. That's why I left it till last."

"You going to tell me what it is or do I have to get rough?"

His surprise flared, faded, a thorough appraisal of her comparative size followed, then a supreme look of masculine superiority. "Ooh, I'm scared."

"Ever heard of wolverines? They make huge grizzlies like you run for cover. Size doesn't matter." It was out before she had a chance to stop it.

The unintended innuendo seemed to have slashed some invisible leash holding him back. Hunger burst in his eyes. He bore down on her, plastering her back against the wall. "It isn't? Maybe I can prove to you just how much it does matter."

Oh, yes, please!

No, moron, no. Don't do this to yourself. He'll hack you to pieces with his whims—his ups and downs. He has serious issues with—heaven knows what. You may have fallen in love with him, but you can't endure his on-off behavior. Not when both modes are so devastating.

Her whole body quivered, beyond her control. Not a good idea if she was supposed to be picking up a scalpel again some time this week. "Draw me diagrams later, OK? If I see you later, that is."

"Oh, you will. I'm right next door to you—again." He caught her back when she tried to walk away. "What's the matter, Cassandra? Can't the queen of tormenting imps handle it?"

"I can handle you any day!" *Get away from him. You're not up to taking him on now.*

"Can you?" He tugged her inside the deserted scrubbing and gowning room. "Can you really, Cassandra?" He locked the door behind them, turned to her, his eyes predatory, starved.

"The surgery…"

"We're waiting for Michael and Phil and the hospital's orthopedic team. The woman has a compound pelvic fracture and we're going to be working simultaneously to minimize anesthesia time." He pulled her to him, ripped the cap off her head, drove his fingers in her hair, held her head, took her lips in one hard, swift kiss. One that stabbed right through her soul. "They'll be a while. I believe you were saying something…?"

She was? When? It felt like she'd never say anything again. He'd changed all the rules, so quickly, so much, she was spinning, not knowing where she was.

"About handling me. You mean the way you did back on the Jet? During our heated…duel?"

Duel was right. They'd almost fought each other for more, deeper, harder. Where that could have led with all those other people on board, she couldn't think.

She couldn't think, period.

"And I won't draw you diagrams 'later'. Now is perfect." He bore down on her and she wriggled out of his reach. The door was locked but it had a glass panel. He caught her.

"Now is crazy, Vidal," she panted, wanting his hands all over her yet trying to pry them off her shoulders, images of people standing outside watching just too sobering.

"*I'm* crazy." The words reverberated against her temple,

her cheek, her throat as his lips roved feverishly over her. "And whose fault is that? How long did you think I could withstand your temptation?"

"It was only twice and I didn't mean—"

"*Only* twice? And you're not counting the time at the airport, huh? Give me a man who would have lasted once. Who wouldn't have pounced on you anyway if given the opportunity, without the least invitation. You're a hazard, Cassandra, to yourself and the world at large." He crushed her to his massive chest, his hands on her buttocks drawing her against his hardness, letting her feel him, measure him. Her resistance lasted another second, then she was wrapped around him, dueling with him again. Kiss for kiss, moan for moan, hard, hot, desperate.

"*Te quiero tanto—tanto*, Cassandra. *Madre de Dios—estoy loco…*"

It was true. He was *really* crazy. Just the thought, the possibility that Cassandra would turn to Karan, or any other man, in frustration had destroyed the last tatters of his sanity, all his misgivings and inhibitions annihilated right along with it. She wanted him? She'd got him. He was taking her. Here. Now.

From an endless distance, sounds—jarring, rattling sounds—filtered in, seeping between her feverish cries and his crashing heartbeats. Then they registered. Jolted him off her.

"Vidal, is that you inside?" Michael's voice came through the door. "The door is stuck. Can you push from your side, see if it will open this way?"

Vidal understood. Michael had seen them, and his overloud speech was meant for the others on the other side of the door. Covering up for them.

Vidal turned to Cassandra, who was still plastered to the wall, panting, shivering. "Go. Scrub and gown, Cassandra. I'll handle this."

He waited until she'd staggered to the sinks, took in a huge breath, and staggered to the door himself.

Half an hour later, sitting at the operating table, Vidal felt Cassandra's approach, called on his long-perfected emotional isolation technique to bar her from his focus. Their patient was there, Joseph already completing her anesthesia and hooking her to the monitors and the ventilatory support. He needed his detachment. Had Cassandra made him lose it forever?

"Is this as bad as it looks?" she gasped. The sight was gasp-worthy indeed.

Grateful for the professional distraction, Vidal handed her the three-dimensional CT scan. "See for yourself."

Cassandra gasped again. "Zygomatic, maxillary, nasoethmoid, internal and external orbital—even mandibular fractures. All incisors, canines and the front molars knocked out. The only facial bone not smashed to smithereens is the frontal bone."

The woman's face was the worst mess he'd ever seen. And that said too much. From her eyebrows down, her face was beyond nightmarish.

"What about her neurological status?" Cassandra asked, as she passed the scans to Phil.

"Amazingly normal. That tough frontal bone must have protected her brain from any direct injury."

"What about indirect, from that brutal blow to her face?" she persisted. "Delayed concussion or worse could still develop!"

"Neurosurgery cleared her for surgery." He gave her a significant look, hoped she'd get the message. She got it— sharp, quick Cassandra, eyes turning turquoise the only sign of her surprise. There hadn't been videotaping in any of the other emergency procedures. Her eyes went to his scrubs, searching for a clip-on microphone, no doubt. When they didn't find one, they swung up, found the omnidirectional microphone hanging from special suspenders and the camera at one wall angled at the operative field of surgical station six.

"So, could you give us some quick notes about advances

in facial trauma reconstruction, be our narrator throughout the surgery, too?'' he prompted.

Cassandra stared at Vidal, unable to hear her own thoughts over the clamor inside her. What had he said? Oh—*oh*!

"Uh, quick notes, sure." She cleared the squeak out of her voice, adjusted her position as she and Vidal started the procedure. "Traumatic complex fractures of the head and face need to be correctly diagnosed and treated or permanent functional and cosmetic deformities will result. During the past decade, accurate diagnosis by two-and three-dimensional CT scans—which have replaced plain X-rays for diagnosis of many types of fracture—and the advent of rigid miniplate fixation have tremendously improved the functional and esthetic results in facial fracture management. Ouch, that wasn't quick after all.''

Michael, who was already working on the woman's unstable pelvic fracture, said, "You're doing fine. Very informative. And what a delivery. You should be making documentaries.''

"Hmm, I'll take that under consideration if I can't find a suitable post back home." She fell silent as she manipulated a cheekbone fragment back into place. After she was done, she retracted the cheek to give Vidal best access as he fixed the miniplate in place, stabilizing the facial buttress.

She went on, "In acute trauma cases like this one, delayed treatment has been replaced by an immediate one-stage repair, applying recent advances in craniofacial techniques, stabilizing the small bone fragments by miniplate fixation and bone grafts, restoring pre-injury facial appearance and function, while at the same time minimizing revisional surgery. Delayed treatment, contrary to common belief, causes far more future problems. However, modern craniofacial surgical techniques are also for patients with pre-existing, post-traumatic facial deformities, no matter how old they are.''

She went on to describe each step of the five-hour operation as they pieced the woman's face back together, her satisfaction rising with each bone back in place, each look into

Vidal's silver eyes. They needed a few fragments for highly crushed bones. With the patient's pelvis already exposed for her second procedure, Michael easily provided them with the bone fragments they needed for grafting.

"As you can see, ten miniplate and screw systems were needed to put the mid-face back together, while Phil used four to stabilize the maxilla." She turned relieved eyes to Vidal, found his intent, blazing, on her. Another buzz of pleasure swept through her. She almost whooped with it as she delivered her closing comment. "A word on expected outcomes, then I promise I'll shut up. It may look a mess beyond hope of healing now, but in a couple of months' time, after all soft tissue swelling and bruising have subsided, Miss Komar will be nearly her old self again."

"Thanks, Cassandra, that was perfect," Vidal drawled, and Cassandra wanted to take his praise right out of his mouth. Literally. "You, too, Phil. A great job as usual. I'll wrap up the video session with a few words about follow-up. You can go."

Cassandra tried to catch his eyes. Didn't he want her to wait for him? Back in her hotel room at least? Didn't he want to pick up where they'd left off?

They didn't pick up where they'd left off.

Vidal didn't even make it to the hotel that night.

She didn't know how long she sat there, waiting, jolting with every imagined sound as she sorted through the first few hundred of their scheduled cases, until exhaustion finally dragged her under, right there on the sofa, into a tormented, tormenting realm of frustration far worse than the previous two weeks.

She woke up, sore and stiff and cranky, to his voice. Over the phone. They talked for over fifteen minutes, but didn't really talk. Vidal only wanted to inform her of the changes to their schedule in Hyderabad, to discuss with her the measures they had to employ to meet their ten-thousand-case quota in their allotted time there. After they'd agreed on a course of action, he told her he'd gather all senior personnel for an eight a.m. meeting.

That was twenty minutes from that now! Including the ten-minute drive to Kishnar Hospital where Vidal had spent the night. She broke all records eating breakfast and zoomed through her morning routine so fast that she actually arrived at the hospital early, and had the luxury of five interminable minutes' loitering outside the meeting room, dreading seeing him again, seeing the coldness back in his expression.

One look into his eyes told her everything.

He wasn't back to being remote and dismissive. His absence last night *had* been beyond his control. Relief uprooted all her inhibitions and she walked right up to him, in front of everyone, hugged him and kissed the first part of him she could reach: his chest where his shirt was unbuttoned.

Vidal's heart tried to burst out of his chest, to meet her lips, smother itself in her kiss.

After a moment of stunned paralysis, peppered by hoots and wolf-whistles from Michael, Phil and Joseph, his arms went around her, lifting her clear off the ground, raising her lips to where they belonged, where he was always dying to have them, right there on his.

He let her slide down his body, sated himself with her eager smile, her open desire, her beauty. *Cielo,* what she was. Unpredictable. Enslaving. How had he lasted so long? How had he doubted her? She wasn't one for playing games. She wanted him and was unashamed to show him, show the world. And had he ever thought her less than the most beautiful woman in creation?

But there was something to take care of first. He looked up, met Karan's eyes, deliberate, triumphant. *See? She's mine. Back off. Or else.*

Karan's eyes were grudging, yet he gave a reluctant, conceding tilt of his raven head. He wanted her: it was a certainty now. Tough. He wasn't getting her, wasn't even coming near her again. Maybe he should take him aside, make sure he understood…

Michael aborted his aggression. "With all of us duly perked up by this unexpected and delightful performance," he said, "don't you think we should get down to some boring business? We didn't meet that seven-hundred patient quota yesterday. Most of our patients yesterday weren't on our lists in the first place. And now, if I understand right, you're saying our work, staying up all night sorting cases, is down the drain."

As everyone's voices rose in complaint, Vidal stepped away from Cassandra, saw her embarrassment, further proof this hadn't been premeditated. The knowledge swelled in his heart. Incredulity too. The whole episode had lasted seconds and an eternity. Time became irrelevant when he entered her orbit. Everything became non-existent. Past and future. Right and wrong and— Arthur…

Work now! Agonize over this later.

He cleared his throat, brought the debate to an end. "Sorry for the setback, but Cassandra and I have already agreed that the only way to deal with this is to sort out everything as we go along, on a daily basis. We'll dedicate three hours first thing each morning to sorting cases and drawing up lists."

Joseph spread his hands in confusion. "But what happened to the old lists?"

"And three working hours gone out of each fourteen? That's a very unproductive way of doing things." That was Karan, raising his eyebrows in subtle antagonism.

Vidal answered Joseph instead. "The lists were of patients rounded up from all over India in anticipation of our arrival. When our schedule went awry, a lot went home and now have to be recalled. There is no control over who will get where when. So the lists are simply outdated. Cassandra and Harry will have their ultra-effective taskforces on the job and they will smooth everything over for you on the medical and administrative level. Apart from that, we'll just have to play it by ear."

As they all grumbled, each in his own way, at the extra

and unexpected workload, Vidal met Cassandra's eyes again, lost all sense of time and place. All sense, period. Again.

He could deal with the next two weeks, work-wise, playing it by ear. He'd been doing it all through this mission. How would he deal with what he felt—with Cassandra?

As it turned out, he didn't have to. Out of extreme necessity, they were never together again for the next two weeks except to work. To deal with all the endless issues that arose, along with their own workload. As the medical co-ordinators of the mission, Vidal, Cassandra and Harry split their sleep time in shifts, never coexisting in the hotel. He couldn't have kept his hands off her otherwise.

When each day ended and he hadn't had the opportunity to act on his cravings, it was a relief. If rending frustration and droning obsession could be called that. Still, it was for the best. If only the rest of the mission could pass like that…

If it did, he'd probably step off the Jet in a straitjacket, spend the rest of his days in a padded room. And if it didn't—that was an even worse fate.

"I still can't believe this!" Cassandra raised her head from the lists in her hand the moment Vidal turned from his conversation with Harry. "We actually did it."

"Yes, we did. Round up the troops, *poca una*. They deserve to know how great they've all been."

"This has been the most chaotic, totally exhausting yet most satisfying time of my life." She beamed up at him, missing him, love for him a blinding pleasure-pain spear lodged all through her. She amended her statement. "Work-wise, that is."

In answer, his eyes crackled silver lightning. Then his hand shot to her head, bracing her for the full measure of his frustration, his hunger. One carnal, clinging kiss that said it all, twisting the spear, driving it deeper.

He stepped away, his eyes filled with storms, only a few within her comprehension. It struck her then. It was beyond his control now, but in his mind he'd rather not come near her. She should save him the fight, the agony, leave him alone. Heaven help her, she couldn't. She wasn't asking for much. Just for anything with him, for any length of time. She had to make that clear.

"Don't frown like that, Vidal. This…" She gestured at herself and the invisible bond between them. "…has no strings attached."

His shutters came down so hard she gasped.

"Let's get this done, Cassandra, or Harry will start loading us with the cargo for always delaying his take-offs."

"What's happening?" Ashley asked Cassandra. "Who are these people?"

Cassandra had wondered herself at the non-Indian-looking men who'd boarded the plane, carrying crates, along with dozens of people transporting their supplies. Her uncomfortable reaction to their presence had made her watch them. Now evidently Ashley felt something too as both Vidal and Harry crossed over to the four men in question, clearly bent on investigating their presence on board the Jet.

It was Vidal Cassandra watched. As she always did. By now she had his every move and expression studied, analyzed, archived. When he wasn't close, dealing with her, she had him figured out. Now his body language spoke of suspicion, antipathy, even suppressed aggression. Her heart itched. What was he picking up from those men? What did he suspect?

Ashley asked again when she didn't answer. "Think there's a problem?"

"I don't know. Maybe there is a problem with maintenance or something, but I'm wondering where—" Words choked as horror detonated. A gun flashed in one man's hand, was shoved between Vidal's eyes. *"No!"*

The man jerked his head, searching for the source of the cry, and Vidal's eyes swung to her, his eyebrows dipping in a severe, urgent signal. *Shut up*, it said. *Don't draw attention to yourself.*

It hadn't even occurred to her to fear for herself. What shut her up, what kept her petrified in her place, was fear for him that that thug might get trigger-happy if he thought anyone was antagonizing him. She wouldn't even breathe until he moved that gun away from Vidal's face.

He didn't. And now his gaze swung back to Vidal, who presented him with that impassive mask that betrayed none of his thoughts or feelings. The man poked his head back hard with the gun, shouted at him and at the security personnel, his English broken but his meaning clear. "I shoot—he—all! Go!"

He shoved Vidal to the area between the crew transportation area and the dental/ophthalmology areas, his colleague holding off the security men, while the other two opened the crates, got out rifles and grenades and handed them around. Then they herded Harry back to the cockpit.

As Vidal approached, the man at his back kept ramming him with the muzzle of his rifle, to establish the upper hand and his willingness to use violence. If not for the weapon at Vidal's back it would have been laughable, that small man hitting and shoving a giant like Vidal. Without the weapon, Vidal could have snapped him in two in a second. But Cassandra knew all too well how a gun made the little gnat invincible, what a bullet could do—and just the thought of Vidal's flesh, his beautiful, precious body being ripped apart by it...

Nausea frothed, rose in a black wave. She beat it back, keeping her eyes on Vidal. He was now giving them all that same silencing stare. *Don't say or do anything*, it said. She almost touched him as he passed her, the need to reassure herself he was here and unharmed, unreasoning, overwhelming. His glare stopped her. *Don't give them more weapons*, it said. *He shouldn't know I'm anything to you.*

You're not anything, her heart wept, *you're everything to me.*

Oh, God, what did these men want?

As soon as the two men had them all rounded up and

covered, the mousy man snapped again, "You move, we shoot."

"Sit!" his companion, a much larger man, roared, pushing Joseph to the floor. He fitted all her conceptions of brutal, mindless enforcers. "All sit!"

Everyone obeyed immediately. She heard Ashley's whimper, Louisa's gasps, Joseph's curse under his breath. Vidal was the only one who didn't make a sound, who wasn't even looking at their hijackers. Wasn't looking anywhere or at anyone either.

"Who's boss?" the brute asked.

Everyone looked at each other, avoiding looking at Vidal. Waiting for him to act as he saw fit, no doubt. He didn't do a thing, kept silent. What was he thinking?

Unable to bear it, afraid that being identified as their boss would put him in more danger, she went against his warning and spoke up. "There's no boss here! This is a humanitarian mission and we're all colleagues doing our jobs. What do you want from us?"

"No boss?" the mouse repeated. Then he gave an odious giggle. "You speak, you boss. You tell them, take orders—or die."

They were in the air. Hijacked.

With a gun to his head, and knowing each of his colleagues had one to theirs, too, Harry had taken off, heading only heaven and those creeps knew where. How they had managed to get past both airport and Jet security with all those weapons and what they really wanted were things they'd only know if the hijackers chose to enlighten them.

They were all still squatting on the floor in rows, all fifty-eight of them. Their hijackers were facing them as they sat in the dentist's chairs, pointing their guns at them.

"What do you think this is all about?" Joseph finally whispered, his brown eyes darting to their jailers to see their reaction. It didn't seem as if they minded that he talked, as long as he didn't move. Joseph got braver. "You think they've made ransom demands by now, or is it the Jet they're after?''

"If they want something, we might get out of this alive. If it's the Jet they want, we're soon going to be extra weight. Dead weight.'' That was Michael.

Phil moved his cramped leg, got a barked order to sit still, raised his hands in a placating gesture and settled back. "Let's not write our epitaphs yet.''

Karan exhaled. "What galls me is that Jet security thought they were just another four people loading our supplies on board, uniforms and badges and all.''

"How do you think they wormed their way into that? And what are we going to do?'' Louisa whispered.

"There must have been someone on the inside helping them in the airport.'' Karan frowned, threw Vidal a disparaging look. "As for what we're going to do, maybe we should ask our boss. Oh, I forgot, we don't have one!''

Cassandra's hackles rose, her whole being in an uproar needing to defend Vidal's inaction. A niggling voice whispered, *But isn't it strange the way he's sitting there, not doing anything? As if he was hiding in anonymity, too scared to move?*

No! What kind of faith did she have in him that he prove himself to her over and over again, only for her to be back to square one in the next crisis, believing the worst of him? Vidal was no coward. Anyway, what could he do now but risk his life with any show of bravado or initiative? She wanted him safe, at any price. Any price at all.

But he was doing something she'd never seen before. Since the moment he'd come to sit among them, he'd managed to—to cloak himself, fade into the crowd, as if he wasn't there. She had to look at him to remind herself he was still among them. And that was saying something, with him the biggest man around, the most distinctive. How did he do that? Why?

"There're only four of them,'' Michael was saying.

"Surely they'll be distracted some time, and then we can strike."

"Maybe they'll fall asleep? Or when they're eating?" Louisa ventured.

"The security men know how to use a gun. If we can manage to get one for them…"

"Listen very carefully, everyone." Vidal didn't look up, his voice no more than a rasp. He still struck them all mute. "You have no idea what kind of people we're dealing with here. I have. At the least sign of heroism, you'll be made an example of."

"Surely they can't fire while we're up here…" Karan started.

Vidal didn't even look at him, yet shut him up somehow. "They may not have done their homework well, since they don't know me, but they're not stupid. We're at an altitude that won't cause decompression if a bullet breaches the Jet's fuselage. So they'll have no qualms about firing. The Jet is their target, us too as the people operating it. They want us alive to serve them. But killing a few of us wouldn't break their hearts."

"How do you know all that?" Cassandra asked, amazed that he sounded so positive.

Vidal still didn't look at her. "They're speaking Badovnan. I've been in Badovna enough in the past few years to know the language fairly well. They belong to a guerilla army that's embroiled in a terrorist war with the provisional Badovnan government on one side and Azernian authorities on the other."

Cassandra's eyes widened in incredulity. Was that what he'd been doing, listening? Shutting everything out as he'd focused on their abductors a few meters away, to catch their conversation? "And they want the Jet as their own private, highly equipped hospital to patch up their war wounded?" she asked.

"That's about it. They decided to hijack us on our way to Uzbekistan, because it's on the same course. So far we're on our flight course, so no one will be the wiser until we pass Uzbekistan.''

"But where are we going to land?" Ashley asked, suppressing a shudder. "How are they going to hide the Jet? Surely we'll be detected."

"They must have a landing site ready," Vidal said. "And it's a country with huge barren and ungoverned areas. A plane, even one the Jet's size, can be hidden easily and never found."

"What good will we be to them when our supplies run out?" Joseph asked.

"They're smugglers and raiders. They'll get us the supplies."

"And how do you know all that?" Karan frowned.

"They belong to the same guerilla army that attacked another GAO convoy in their region a few months ago. They abducted a friend of mine, the mission head in the Balkans at the time, Lorenzo Banducci, if you've heard of him. I'm sure that's how they always get their medical needs. They just got a little more ambitious this time."

They all fell silent. Forever, it seemed. The two armed men were eating, getting louder. Sniggering at them.

Cassandra closed her eyes. Those weren't people. They were monsters. There still had to be a way out. Vidal knew so much, maybe he'd know that, too. "So what do you advise we do, Vidal?"

"He can advise nothing," Karan snarled. "They're not just any hijackers, they're part of an organized army with a chaotic, lawless country to take refuge in. As usual, the world will know when it's too late to do anything about it. And I'm damned if I wait until we're in their stronghold, and be their slave for the rest of my life. I'd rather die now."

"No one's going to die, and no one's going to be—"

"Enough, Vidal," Michael growled. "Don't start giving us promises and false hope. I'm with Karan. There'll be no negotiation with these mercenaries, no way out. It's do or die."

''Michael, Karan, no!'' Vidal looked up now, tried to exert his will on the agitated men. ''I have a plan…''

But it was too late. In slow-motion horror, Cassandra saw Karan standing up, then Michael, the two hijackers jumping to their feet, shouting, rifles cocking. Michael pointed to the toilets and food and the hijackers got louder, came forward, jabbing at him with their rifles to drive him down. Karan jumped on the bigger man, on the gun, Michael wrestled with the smaller one. Screams. Vidal's shouts. People throwing themselves on the floor, hands over their heads. Cracks of thunder and fire, deafening, heart-bursting. Blood. Spraying her face, hot, corrosive. Three people falling to the ground in bloody heaps.

Then Vidal collapsed over her.

CHAPTER EIGHT

"STAY down, stay down." The soundless words hissed in her ear, over and over. Spilling from Vidal's mouth.

Oh, God, oh, God—his breathing erratic—his heartbeat rocking her. And that sticky heat on her back...

A third armed man had come running from the cockpit and stood with the other two, shouting at their captives, kicking them as they lay on the floor, jabbing them with their rifles, forcing them to sit up. Forcing Vidal off her.

It was then she saw it. Blood splashed over his chest. The world churned as her lifeforce drained. "Vidal..."

They'd shot him. Now they had to shoot her, too.

"Cassandra..." He could still talk. She could still save him. She snatched her consciousness back, started to rise to her knees. He clung to her. "That's Michael's blood."

Really? "And you...?" Her lips moved. No sound came. He understood.

"Fine," he mouthed.

That was all she needed to know. Now she could think of others.

Michael. Karan. Louisa. Lying there, their ripped flesh wide open, draining their lifeblood away.

"*You!*" she shouted. The three hijackers turned their heads to her.

Vidal crushed her hand in his, trying to make her stop, sit down. She wouldn't.

"Are you crazy?" She made the universal gesture beside her head. "Those people you shot are the chief doctors you need. This one..." she pointed to Michael "...is the one who gets your bones fixed..." She pointed to her arms and legs, made a pantomime of breaking something. "That one is the

126

one who will take care of your women and get you babies. And this woman is the one who will keep you alive after you have surgery.'' She was on her feet now, yelling. ''Do you understand me?''

The third man clearly did. He turned to the other two and let rip a torrent of Badovnan. Then he turned to her. ''Are they dead?''

She didn't need a second invitation. In under a minute she'd examined the three of them. Michael was barely alive, the other two critical. She turned on the hijackers, frantic. ''We need to operate—*now*! We still might be able to save them. Or we can tell your superiors how you killed the doctors they need!''

''You surgeon?''

''Yes. And I will need my team to get up and come assist me. *Now*, do you understand?''

Another clamor among the hijackers, then the man nodded. ''Who do you need?''

She pointed at the surgical nurses. ''Those four to prepare for the surgery.'' Then she pointed to Joseph and Vidal. ''The man with the brown eyes and hair, my anesthetist; the big man, my surgical nurse. We will operate first on Michael, *that* one. I need my emergency doctors to take care of the other two until I finish. These two women and this man. Now get out of my way.''

Under tight gun cover, the people who were allowed to rise erupted into action, their practiced routine fueled by desperation for their colleagues, reaching superhuman levels of efficiency.

Cassandra cast a look at Vidal as he and Joseph prepared Michael for the emergency thoracotomy. Before all this had happened, he'd said he had a plan. Did he really? And would it still work now?

''Gigli saw—and get me another two lines into him. Central access. Blood only. Joseph, suction the blood more from his trachea, then suction the operative field when I open him up.''

Cassandra's rapid-fire demands penetrated Vidal's rage.

Seeing Michael lying there, his chest blown open by two point-blank bullets... He wanted to forget about all his careful plans to lie low, divert them, lead them on and then strike when they least expected it. He wanted to attack them, roaring and frothing, take their bullets full in his chest, and snap their necks with his last breath. And if Cassandra hadn't been there, his magnificent lioness who was still protecting him, hiding his identity, in the way of stray bullets, as Louisa had been... *Madre de Dios*, Louisa!

Focus. Only Michael mattered now.

He snapped the saw into Cassandra's anxious hands then dealt with her other demands in seconds.

Joseph reported Michael's status as she checked the saw, revved it. ''He has Beck's triad, Cassandra.'' Beck's triad, or acute compression triad, meant increased jugular venous pressure, hypotension, and diminished heart sounds. ''He's deteriorating—too fast, dammit!'' Joseph muttered.

She chopped a nod, divided the sternum. ''He has cardiac tamponade.'' Blood was filling the heart's covering, the pericardium, stopping it from pumping. Rapidly fatal. ''Not sure if this is a cardiac or great vessel injury. We'll see—right away.''

Vidal's hair stood on end again, watching her moves. Decisive, fluent, ultra-efficient. In her element now, fully in charge. He'd already watched her perform the posterolateral thoracotomy. Watched those small hands incising the skin from the border of the sternum to the mid-axillary line, reaching the intercostal muscles, incising those with a lightning succession of scalpel, heavy scissors and blunt dissection, inserting the rib spreaders between the ribs and opening Michael's chest up. But she'd needed more exposure. Now she had it, moving the rib spreader to the midline, exposing almost all of Michael's chest organs so she could get to the injury and perform everything at once. Resuscitate by relieving the tamponade, diagnose the extent of injuries—and treat them.

Cassandra made a small incision in the pericardium with scissors, then tore it longitudinally with her fingers, evacuating the blood.

''No response,'' Joseph hissed, after he'd suctioned it

Vidal heard the terrible sound of Cassandra's grinding teeth. ''He's got a right ventricular injury, an aortic one, too.'' Cassandra shot her eyes up to him. ''Vidal, your finger is bigger. Put it here, block the wound. Dick…'' She turned to the real surgical nurse helping them. ''Non-absorbable, polypropene sutures.''

''Will you suture the injury directly or do you need to do a bypass?'' Vidal asked, his whole being revolting at having his finger driven into his friend's barely beating heart, feeling the man's life blowing past in a storm, with him useless, trying and failing to dam the flood.

''No—no need. Teflon pledgets, though.'' She snatched both articles from Dick, and quickly closed the cardiac injury with mattress sutures to avoid obstructing coronary flow, then turned to the aortic injury, performing the aortic repair in under a minute.

''Nothing's working.'' Joseph was panting now. ''His blood pressure is still unrecordable. Entering ventricular tachycardia.''

''He might have deeper or lower injuries. Stop all fluids,'' Cassandra cried. ''Cross-clamps!'' Cross-clamping the thoracic aorta and blocking it diverted blood from the rest of the body and redistributed it to the coronary vessels, lungs and brain to reduce bleeding out from injuries in the lower torso. But it meant fluid resuscitation had to be stopped as it would only cause overload in those vital areas, hastening heart failure.

She cross-clamped the aorta at the level of the diaphragm to maximize blood flow to the spinal cord, waited a few seconds, her eyes clinging to the monitor for any sign of stabilization. Michael only flatlined.

"No, no, Michael!" she shouted, dipping both her hands in his chest for double-handed direct cardiac massage. "Come back. Come *back*, damn you!"

Michael didn't come back.

Ten minutes later, they were all standing there, petrified, Cassandra's hand still holding Michael's inert heart, the only sounds in the whole Jet the loud drone of the engine and her choppy sobbing.

Vidal's heart was bursting with wrath and futility, spilling venom and vengeance into his system.

Those monsters would pay.

He raised his eyes to Cassandra, experiencing her devastation but dreading witnessing it. The sight of her struck another crippling blow to his chest. Her face rigid, not contorting with her sobs, eyes wide and streaming, seeking his, begging for him to share the agony, halve it.

"Cassandra…" His hands went to her shaking ones, removing them from inside Michael's chest.

Her mask trembled violently with her trembling chin. "Louisa—Karan. I have to save them!"

"You will."

And she did. Two hours later, both Louisa and Karan were stable and in Recovery. Louisa had a messy shoulder wound with a severed axillary artery and nerve, which had needed both Cassandra's and Vidal's expertise with trauma surgery and microsurgery respectively. Karan had a torn liver and abdominal aorta, injuries right up Cassandra's alley.

All through both procedures, Dick hadn't dried her sweat but her tears. They had been all that had showed of her turmoil. Her hands had been steady, her mind clear, her decisions unerring.

Now the hijackers herded them back with the rest of the personnel and the crew, the man who spoke good English warning them against any more attempts.

Vidal would have given his soul to be able to take her in his arms, comfort her. If he could have given her the time to wallow in shock and grief… He couldn't. He had to act now. In one more hour at most they would be landing in Badovna, and then it would be too late.

He inclined his head to the man beside him, one of the flight crew, murmured something to him. The man mirrored the gesture, nodded, said something that didn't make sense. It was obviously an indication that he understood, but was phrased so the hijackers would think they were discussing something innocuous..

"Cassandra, I'm talking to you but don't give any outward indication that I am. When you want to answer, pretend that you're talking to Ashley."

She remained inert by his side, only the quickening of her breathing indicating that she'd heard him.

"About my plan. The small man, he'd love to kick my ass. The big one wants to measure himself up against me, too."

"How do you know that?"

"It's a male thing, hard to explain. When I asked what they were still doing on board in the beginning, I gave them the kind of look men take to their grave. That's why I shut down after I knew what they were. To give them the satisfaction of thinking me cowed, make them all cocky and appeased, to eliminate me as a threat in their minds and stop me being the trigger of any deranged behavior. *Dios*, if only Michael and Karan had waited…"

He bit back the words, exhaled. "Anyway, I grew up on the streets with their like, Cassandra. I survived by studying them and making use of all their petty inferiority and superiority complexes and stupidities. I'm going to use theirs to create a safe diversion. Then we can—"

She interrupted him, voice quivering. "What if you're wrong? What if they just shoot you, too?"

"They won't. I'll give them too good a time humiliating me, give them the shovel to dig their own graves. Don't worry, I did it almost every day until I was thirteen. How do you think I survived being among all those adult and mostly psychotic thugs?"

"Oh, God, Vidal, if this is some wacky, macho idea…"

"No, it isn't. But I need your help to pull it off. We don't have much time. If we land in Badovna, it will be all over."

"OK, OK. What's your plan?"

"Here it is…"

"I need to see our patients."

The three men looked at Cassandra, each saying something clearly rude, looking her up and down and snickering.

"Please, you have to listen to the doctor." Vidal rose after her, keeping a footstep behind, his voice and body language very convincingly subservient.

"She your boss?" the mouse sniggered, jumping at the bait as Vidal had predicted, salivating at the chance to humiliate him.

Vidal bowed his head more. "Yes. She knows what she's talking about. The patients can still die if she doesn't check on them, give them the necessary drugs."

The men looked at each other, then gave her the go-ahead.

The man with good English rose, smirked at Vidal's bowed head. "You all tail between your legs now. You all big and strong in the beginning."

"S-sorry. She sent me to see who you were. I—I follow orders," Vidal stuttered. "You—you do, too…"

"Not woman orders, sissy." The good-English man guffawed.

This the other two understood, and loved. Their raucous laughter rose.

"Come here, sissy," the brute said.

Cassandra's heart ricocheted inside her as she loaded the syringes.

The abuse was starting. His plan was working so far. What if it got out of hand?

"W-what are you going to do to me?" Vidal's deep voice had that weird, authentic tremor to it. How did he manage to act so well? She *knew* he wasn't afraid of them. Not for himself. Yet he played the spineless part perfectly.

"You afraid, sissy? We just teach you a little lesson!"

That was her cue. At least, she thought it was. She just couldn't take any more.

Cassandra turned. "One more thing—the copilot, he's diabetic. If he doesn't have his insulin now he'll go into a coma. I'll go give him his injection…"

"Why didn't *he* say something?" the good-English guy asked, suspicious.

Cassandra looked heavenwards. "You think he'll try to talk to the man who has a gun to his head?"

"*You* talk!"

"I know you won't kill me, I'm too valuable."

"We won't kill *him*. Not when we're still up here!" He translated to the other two and they all snorted with laughter again.

"If it's OK with you, I'll go to him now."

"What if trick?" the brute said.

Cassandra huffed, "Oh, for heaven's sake! What happened to the big men with the guns? Afraid of a tiny woman with a syringe?"

Another exchange of uncertain looks, then good-English man talked into the intercom. "Copilot, come here!"

"I don't know why you won't let me go to him—" Cassandra started to protest.

"He comes here. Now you shut up."

The moment Sean passed Vidal on his way to Cassandra, Vidal, who'd been standing with his head bowed, suddenly raised his eyes to them, uncoiling to his full height, spreading his awesome physique, towering over them. "You should be polite to women, you know."

The men did a double-take, sheer surprise replaced by instant rage in their eyes.

"Lesson time, *sissy*," the good-English guy snarled. "You don't talk until we talk to you, and you only say yes, please, and master."

"Oh? That's what *you* say to *your* masters while they're...?"

He made an explicit gesture, the expression on his face pure derogatory malice. And the three men exploded in his face, swinging at him with their rifles with bone-crushing force. He fell instantly, his huge body hitting the floor with a sickening thud that would forever echo in Cassandra's mind.

She knew nothing more. Someone was running, screaming Vidal's name.

Then she crashed to her knees beside Vidal, heard the broken, enraged English of his attackers. *Vidal, Vidal!* Only his name made sense. Only the blood pouring from his mouth. His closed eyes.

Flailing hands checked his pulse. Then she swung around, rabid, screaming, "*You killed him!*"

That froze them. Then the mouse kicked him hard to make sure. Vidal remained death-flaccid.

"Dick, Joseph..." Cassandra screamed again. "Come here, carry him to the resuscitation area. We'll shock him."

"Now listen here..." The good-English guy's voice rose

"*No! You* listen here. Your bosses want doctors and nurses. How will they punish you if we tell them you've killed him for fun? Because you got angry? A man who could save hundreds of your brothers-in-arms? We can still save him."

The men fidgeted, looked at each other, gave grudging nods.

Joseph and Dick struggled to carry Vidal's limp body to the resuscitation suite. Cassandra ran after them, preparing the external defibrillation device, charging it to maximum.

The three men ran after them and stood close, watching, the last keeping the hostages covered as Dick and Joseph frantically cut off Vidal's clothes, exposing his chest.

"You bastards!" Cassandra shouted again. "If this doesn't work..."

"We didn't hit him that hard!"

"No? You're saying you didn't do *this*?"

The men instinctively leaned closer together to inspect the damage they'd done—and she moved. Without a second's hesitation. Slammed the defibrillator paddles on the one closest to her. The electric charge crackled from the brute to the mouse, and in a second they were both twitching on the floor. The third man didn't have a second to react, with Vidal's feet simultaneously and explosively ramming him, slamming the rifle out of his hand, smashing full strength into his face. He dropped like a bag of bricks.

Dick and Joseph jumped on them instantly, stabbing them with the narcotics Cassandra had loaded and left ready for them.

Vidal bolted off the resus table to his feet, snatching her into his arms, crushing her to him over the fallen bodies of their abusers.

He'd done it. *He'd done it!* But...

"One left!" Vidal's growl as he let her go filled her with awe, and pride. She couldn't wait for him to fulfill the threat his tones carried. "Everybody, get something to restrain those bastards with. Security, any of them tries anything again, use whatever force you think is necessary."

He stalked to the flight crew's station, picked up the mike of the intercom system with the cockpit. "I'm sure you heard it all, dear hijacker. Now we're armed and we're many and, believe me, we're very, very angry. You only have the pilot to threaten, whom you can't shoot if you want to land in one piece. You have three choices—harm him and kill us all, kill yourself, or get out here and surrender."

There was silence on the other side, then Harry's voice crackled. "He's gesturing that he doesn't understand."

Vidal's huge shoulders rose in a move eloquent of barely leashed fury. He said a few words in Badovnan, then he ended, "And I have a hunch you did understand me the first time. So here's the deal, you little piece of slimy trash. If you don't come out now, I promise, when you do, and you will, I will break every bone in your body. All two hundred and five of them. That includes each bone in your back and neck. You've seen me, you know I can do it and, believe me, I'll do it with surgical precision, so that you won't die. I'm a surgeon after all.''

In a minute, the man came out of the cockpit, to find Vidal, Dick, and Joseph each pointing a rifle at him. He raised his hands in the air, his rifle above his head. Cassandra watched Vidal walking up to him, taking the rifle out of his hands and stripping him of the grenades and every other weapon on his person. Then he stood back, facing him. For a long moment, everyone held their breaths. Then Vidal exploded into action, swinging his arm back and out, the back of his balled fist catching the man on the side of his head with a loud crack. The man fell in a limp heap over the seats, then didn't move again.

Cassandra ran to Vidal, threw herself at his back, hugged him with all her love and horror and relief. He turned, pulled her under his arm, clasped her to his side and rushed into the cockpit.

Harry turned to them, his eyes shimmering.

''It's over.'' Vidal placed his hand on Harry's shoulder.

''Yes. Thank God. Thanks to you two. We could hear everything—all the time. Michael—oh, God—Michael and the others. And I was so afraid for you, for everyone out there. I felt so helpless I thought I'd have a heart attack...''

Vidal squeezed his shoulder harder. ''It's over, Harry. *Over*. Make your reports and then we're canceling the mission to Uzbekistan. I can't ask our volunteers to function after this. Take us somewhere where they can recover. Somewhere from where we can send Michael's body home.''

They landed in Badovna after all for a brief hour to deliver the hijackers to the Badovnan government. Then they refueled and charted a new course to London.

All through the flight to Badovna, the meeting with the officials there, the time spent rechecking Louisa and Karan and implementing their post-operative routines, Vidal had kept Cassandra glued to his side. Not that he'd needed to. She hadn't allowed an inch between them either, clinging to his hand, burrowing into him as if trying to hide inside him. As he wanted—to hide her inside him, to hide inside her.

After the plane took off for London and someone had removed the meal they couldn't eat, she surged into him again, shuddering when his arms squeezed her to him full strength.

"Vidal—what happens now?"

"We mourn, we deal with it, then we go on."

Tears surged, spilled again. "Nothing like this has ever happened to me, Vidal. I've never seen violence up this close, never knew desperation, never lost people…this close, this way…"

He had. He'd known violence and desperation since the day he'd opened his eyes to the world. To a father who'd knifed him to get him to hand over the cents he'd kept from his con jobs and a mother who'd bashed his head against the wall when she'd run out of booze. By the age of nine he'd had enough, had run away, lived on the streets. And there he'd known every other sort of violence, seen every sort of atrocity, experienced every sort of loss. Losing friends bleeding to death on pavements or going spastic on overdoses in gutters. Losing innocence, hope—losing his very soul…

His hug tightened until she whimpered, yet crushed herself harder to him. *Lighten it up. Pull her back from the precipice. Heal her.* He raised her face to him, smiled into her shimmering eyes. How beautiful they were. How much they meant. Everything. The heart he'd thought had burst with fear for her burst again with too much emotion. "The way you handled the whole thing, it looked like you handled life-and-death situations every day. You were incredible, unbelievable. *Querida*, you can never know how proud I am of you!"

"*You* were incredible and unbelievable—and more. I still can't get my head around what you did, how you came up with it, what an actor you are, how fearless, how—"

"Fearless? Me? What about you, Ms stared-the-monsters-down-and-got-them-doing-my-bidding? Ms zapped-the-monsters-loaded-with-guns-and-grenades? Nothing I came up with would have meant a thing without you carrying it out so perfectly. Talk about keeping your cool under fire. When they knocked me down and you ran screaming, I knew we'd get the bastards for sure. They fell for it completely. You convinced them I'd died and—''

"Don't say it—ever again,'' she choked. "And it wasn't acting. I was scared out of my mind. You hit the floor so hard, lay there so flaccidly, and the—the blood pouring from your mouth…'' A violent shudder engulfed her

He soothed her, smoothed her hair, absorbed her shudders. "I told you I'd roll with their blows…''

"It didn't seem you'd rolled with anything. I saw them swing their rifles and I even heard them connect, and you went down like a felled tree and lay there on the floor, looking…'' She choked again, buried her face in his throat, her hot, ragged breath snatching at his soul.

"I did roll with the blows. They barely touched me—at least, nothing breakable or vital. Another thing I learned on the streets…'' And at home. "How to sustain the least amount of damage, live to fight—every day. And I told you I'd bite my inner lip on purpose, make myself bleed, convince them they'd pounded me.''

She winced, shuddered again. Then her eyes widened. "Does it hurt?''

"What?''

"Your lip!''

"I haven't thought about it…'' He touched his tongue to the tattered flesh he'd ripped apart, experimenting. "I guess it does—some.''

"Can I make it better?'' She licked her lips, made him feel he was the most luscious thing she'd ever seen, the only thing that would quench her cravings. Her eyes, blasting blue fire, told him more, told him everything. "Please?''

He groaned, crushing her lips, knowing that this time there was no turning back.

He was taking her, giving himself to her, here, now. Even if the world ended.

Cassandra cried out as his mouth crashed down on hers. Then again with each restless shift, each urgent plunge. Her tongue searched for his injury, soothed and sobbed. Then he took over, taking the kiss from pain to passion. And it was poignant. Connecting with him again, knowing he was here, alive, powerful—unharmed. The man she'd been born to love.

They were fighting again, struggling for deeper, closer. She was sobbing, tears streaming, incoherencies spilling into his mouth. Survival, frustration, lust, love—now. *Now.*

But he was wrenching his lips from hers, her arms from his body, casting her out, away again. No—he couldn't be so cruel. Her fists pummeled him, hands clawing at him. *Come back. Come back and devour me again, let me devour you. Prove you're alive, I'm alive. Let me taste your life, give you mine. Let me love you.*

"*Vidal!*"

He erupted to his feet. "I can't survive this any more, Cassandra."

She searched his face. Saw her frenzy reflected back at her in his every quivering muscle. She still wanted confirmation, a promise. "When we reach London…?"

He shuddered. "I can't last till London, *querida*—I won't! *Now*, Cassandra—no more waiting."

Yes! choked on her lips. A last flicker of sanity struck. Her eyes darted around. Everyone was awake, unable to settle down, tension still crackling.

He bent, branded her lips again. "Go to the toilet—I'll catch up."

Heartbeats set off like a firecracker. What he'd suggested was audacious, and if anybody found out, terminally embarrassing.

How come she hadn't thought of it first?

Anywhere, anytime, anything. With him.

She staggered to her feet, his eager strength boosting her

limp muscles. She caught his face in her hands, her lips opening on his again, a giggle of exhilaration and unbearable anticipation escaping. The look in his eyes was worth dying for. *He* was worth dying for.

"Go, *querida*. Give me two minutes."

"And no more!"

Excitement warred with co-ordination, and won. Her walk to the toilet proved to be the hardest physical task she'd ever performed, with her bones turned to rubber. She half fell into the small compartment and her heart lurched with disappointment. Would Vidal fit in there with her?

She couldn't believe they were doing this!

But they would and she couldn't wait.

She didn't have to. His peremptory rap came the moment she closed the door. He hadn't been two minutes. Or he had and it was she who'd spent them swaying in the aisles. Then he was there, filling the compartment, filling her heart and reason and world. She opened her arms as wide as her need.

Vidal had never thought he'd see heaven. Not in this life, not in the next. But there it was, what he'd never believed in, what he'd never deserved, standing before him, welcoming, living, breathing…

Dios, living and breathing! It could have been her lying torn in resuscitation now. Lying dead…

He snatched at her, snatched at her clothes, an inhuman sound issuing from him. A continuous growl, a backlash of terror, a frenzy of relief, a craze of passion.

She grabbed at him too, at his zipper. Hers snagged in his feverish fingers. He tugged at them, aggressive now. "Skirts, *mi amor*, wear skirts…"

Her ravenous sobs turned to giddy giggles, spiking his heat, feeding his frenzy. The creamy limbs he bared writhed under his touch, helping him, kicking away their shackles. On his knees, cramped, back against the wall, he captured them, worshipping, feasting, sinking his teeth in their resilience. Her cries filled his mind, fueled his insanity. Control receded, then she moaned and it disappeared altogether.

"Just come inside me—now, Vidal, now!"

Flashing blue and yellow filled his eyes. A stroke? Now, that would be heaven. To die in her arms, buried inside her. He freed himself, his lurching fingers fumbling with the protection he'd gone in search of.

"No, don't!" Her lips sank into his neck, feeding at his pulse, her fingers fighting his for it, flinging it away.

"Protection..." he panted.

She suckled his flesh harder. "I'm...protected."

"You mean..." The Pill? Or something else? Why?

"Yes!" She squashed herself to his erection, rubbing, whimpering. "Oh, you're killing me..."

Thoughts, the twinge of disappointment, vanished. He lifted her, perched her on the sink's edge, lips savage, hands rough, spreading her over his hips, filling his hands with her flesh, squeezing hard, the growling back, filling his throat. Then he plunged into her. Fierce and full. Invading, overstretching the hot, live honey that was her. Engulfed, consumed in her clenching hunger. At last. *At last.*

It took no more than that. One thrust. Hypercharged nerves discharged. Her satin screams echoed his roars, her body convulsed along with his in a paroxysm of release, one sustained seizure that destroyed the world around them.

Time no longer registered. Nothing did. Nothing existed. Only being merged with her, pouring himself into her, feeling her around him, inside and out.

Dios, it had been beyond control. Desperate, abrupt, climactic. Release of all pent-up cravings and frustrations and terror. And it had been...beyond description. It had been everything, yet not enough. Would anything ever be?

The blinding pleasure was already draining, pangs of withdrawal intensifying, tension roaring up his awareness pathways again. *More*, it screamed, *all*. Her, them, like this. Like *this*... He thrust deeper into her. Her cry went through his brain, scorched its way to his loins.

But was it a cry for more, too? Were her body's contractions around his the throb of satisfaction or frustration or, worst of all, pain?

He withdrew, dread riding him, every snatched breath driving her further into his bloodstream, and saw Cassandra, everything his fantasies never dared invent, wrapped around him, face transfigured by ebbing pleasure, by renewed madness. She dragged him closer, clenched around him, and her trembling lips, red and swollen, spilled her urgent demand into his. "Vidal— Oh, darling—again, *please*!"

That was everything. "*Si, mi amor*. Yes, again—and again…" He fused their lips, dueled with her again for a faster descent into delirium. As before, their mating shot from fierce to ferocious. But it wasn't like before. This time, plundering her depths, being consumed by her, went on and on, over and over, pleasure not a sudden annihilating blast but heightening, accumulating, promising even more destruction. Was she feeling the same?

"*Please…*" Her plea was pained and fear flashed into his mind. Her delicate flesh and the hard, steel surfaces in this damned cramped space, even with his cushioning hands and arms…

"*Querida*, what…?"

"Just—just— Oh, darling, it's too much, just *give* me— Oh-h…"

So it was the same with her, equal desperation for release. He let go, picked up speed, gave it to her. The storm that had been building since they'd met again reached its crescendo as she climaxed around him, her agonized satisfaction wringing his own, milking him of every drop of pleasure.

Someone knocked on the door.

Dios! Why did the world still exist?

Still joined, still shuddering in the aftermath, he gathered her fully to him and she clung back. He carried her, rocking her, soothing. "Shh, take your time—they can wait."

The knock came again, impatient this time. And this time Cassandra moved, spilled out of his arms. Separation jolted through him, through her, too, it seemed. A choked chuckle escaped her. "I guess they can't." She bent to her clothes, swayed. He swore.

"*Infierno!* There are three more toilets!" He was on his knees, helping her dress, needing one more caress, one more taste of those thighs that had cradled him all the way to heaven. She dragged him up and hugged him with all her strength. Then she smiled up at him and all the chambers of his heart melted into one useless space.

"How are we going to get out now?" she asked, flushed, still panting.

"We'll just walk out. Anyone who wants to make something of it can take me on."

"After the compound fractures you gave the hijackers, I don't think anyone will take you on, ever again. *I* will, though. I'll take you on—any way at all." His body obeyed again, hardened with her promise, and she pressed another abandoned kiss on his lips. "OK, I'm ready."

That was Cassandra, surprising the hell out of him yet again. He'd expected her to blush and ask him to leave first, divert whoever it was until she slipped out. But she was the one who opened the door, smiled at the first disgruntled then stunned Dick, then walked ahead of him to their seats, her wobbling steps the only sign of her upheaval.

As he dropped by her side, his blood felt too thick for his heart to push through his veins. Aftershocks were still rocking him as hard as the need to remain connected with her. Mercifully, she surged into him again, hugged him and rested her head on his heart.

A heart that was shrinking with impending doom.

She was being too...blithe about it all. Was she used to this? Was this why she was on birth control months after the break-up of her last relationship—because casual sex was a normal practice in her life? Casual sex, anywhere?

She'd said she'd take him on, any way at all. For how long?

Por Dios, why was he wondering and agonizing over it when he knew the answer? It wouldn't be for long. And even if she didn't break it up soon, he would.

He had to.

CHAPTER NINE

"ARE you telling me it's over?"

Cassandra looked down at Vidal as he lay sprawled beneath her, magnificent, vital—oh, but he was so aptly named, her Vidal—and big, big enough to sleep on comfortably. Not that she'd slept. Vidal had kept her up all night. She'd kept him up, too...

"Ask me that in a couple of weeks." He moved, eased her onto her back and leaned half over her, a hair-roughened, heavily muscled thigh driving between hers. She clung immediately, arching, opening, accommodating him, fierce delight stabbing her at feeling him hot and hard and heavy against her again.

"What happens in a couple of weeks?" She bit into his pectoral muscle, delirious with the long-craved freedom, drawing his rumbles of pleasure.

"I may be able to think again then." He rubbed his body down hers, slow, deliberate, abrading her every nerve end into a riot. "Though I doubt it."

"OK, let me make the question easier." Her teeth scraped along his collar-bone to his steely deltoid, sinking in, tapping into his virility, his power. Her satisfied smile spread on his flesh when she felt his powerful response, heard it, smelled it. "Is the Jet Hospital's mission aborted?"

She knew he'd understood her the first time. Now she waited for his answer, watching the shadows flitting over his beloved face as he withdrew slightly to look at her. She didn't understand any of them, only knew that the sheer intensity of passion and appreciation she was already addicted to had changed back to the brooding she dreaded.

Though, she had to admit, he looked fantastic, brooding.

He looked fantastic anyway, every way. But when he was above her, inside her, steel eyes burning, face taut with need, seized in ecstasy, driven, dark then ardent, protective in the blissful aftermath…his beauty was painful to behold. And she'd thrown herself into the agony.

Those gifted fingers combed her hair, raised thick locks, sifting them and letting them fall to her breast over and over again, hypnotizing her. "After what happened, we have to touch base with GAO central offices, both here in London and back in LA, investigate how it happened, how we can make sure it never happens again. We also have to see who still wants to be on the mission."

"I do." Did she sound too anxious?

She bet she did, if the flare in his eyes was anything to go by. What was he thinking? Was he thinking at all beyond the present? He'd already said he wasn't.

He smoothed the back of his hand down her cheek, and back up again. "You may want to take a few days, let this sink in, take the decision later."

She pressed her face into his hand, like a petting-hungry cat. "What happened won't stop me from continuing the mission, Vidal. It was an accident…"

"Oh, no, it wasn't. It was a crime and it was made possible by many people's negligence. Mine in part."

"Oh, no, you don't. You're not going on that guilt trip. I won't let you."

"It's not a guilt trip, it's the truth. As mission leader I should have—"

She sat up abruptly, shoving him again onto his back, loomed over him, the need to hit him, for being so—so *stupid* crackling. "You're the medical mission leader. Security wasn't at any time part of your job. And that, sir, is the end of that."

His lids slid down, hiding his expression, his descending brows darkening it even more. "One can rationalize anything if—"

She cut him off again, sighing. "Anyway, I'm the one

who's guilty. I'm responsible for Michael's death—it was me who failed to save him!''

His expression was simplicity itself to read now. Incredulous fury. ''What idiocy is that? No one could have saved him. He took two point-blank large-caliber, high-velocity projectiles right in his heart. That he survived long enough for you to attempt emergency surgery is the miracle.''

''I know that. I'm gutted over what happened to him, over losing him, I'll always relive the horror and desperation I felt as he slipped through my fingers, but I'm *not* feeling guilty. It was beyond me. Like the hijacking was beyond you.'' One mocking eyebrow rose, head going to one side, hair falling with a thud over his shoulder. ''But you see how anyone can twist anything to wallow in self-blame?''

He held her eyes for a protracted moment, the intensity she depended on surging back into his. Then he breathed a husky ''Point taken—and conceded,'' and turned his face into her hair, breathed in the newly shampooed fragrance. The fragrance he'd put there, in their presidential suite's incredible Jacuzzi, right after he'd made love to her there.

Coming to this suite had been beyond her wildest dreams. The unbridled night of passion they'd shared there had felt like a magical wedding night, but she'd still protested at the extravagance. The suite cost almost as much as the rest of the mission's whole accommodations. He'd just shrugged. After all they'd been through, what better time than now for a treat? When she'd asked why he hadn't gotten them out of that hellhole in Casablanca, he'd said the other options had been to stay in Casablanca's top hotels. Not fair to the rest of the crew! With the mission interrupted, they were no longer part of a team, on their own time and at their own expense. His, that is...

''Fire.'' He rubbed his face into her hair, rumbling. ''Fire spun solid, just as gorgeous and bewitching and dangerous. Your body, too. And your spirit.''

Her heart lurched with pleasure and pride. ''Ooh, that's so...poetic.''

"Not at all. It's how I see you."

"Fair enough. I see you as a force of nature, too."

He laughed. She pressed the wonderful sound between her memory's pages. "Earth, wind, or water?"

She bent to his smile, put her tongue to that sharp canine she'd memorized. "A mix of all three, with a huge dose of lightning thrown in!"

That lightning struck her again as he heaved up, his lips claiming hers, pushing her back, spreading her, then drawing back to look his fill. Once he had her hyperventilating, he let his large, virtuoso hands possess breasts aching with too much pleasuring, hard and burning for more. His awesome head bent to them, this time soothing the hurt of his earlier possession, the hurt she'd inflicted on herself in her abandon, begging him, pummeling him for *harder*. He licked the swollen, hardened nipples, capturing them in gentle, moist kisses, until she was begging again.

She drove her itching hands through his luxurious hair, clawed at him, breath burning, his scent and taste, his sound and sight permeating her, embedded in her body and soul forever. "Stop torturing me, Vidal. Just fill me…"

He resisted her, raised his head, and his male-who-knows-he-pleasures-his-woman-out-of-her-mind smile sent another liquid rush of madness gushing inside her. "Let me feast, *amor*. I've done nothing but pounce on you, tear away as few clothes as I could off you to be able to bury myself inside you…"

"You tore them *all* away last night." And he had, literally. The moment they'd stepped into the suite. He seemed to have a particular grievance against her jeans.

"I did, to feel you beneath me, rub all of me against all of you and go crazy feeling all that fragrant, hot, supple satin writhing around me, cushioning me, enfolding me. Now it's time to explore, savor, study…"

By the time he was done, he had enough data about her every inch, her every response, to fill volumes. Not to mention the discoveries he'd made about erogenous zones she'd never known she had. He taught her something new with every touch. He taught her what feeling exquisite, feeling wholly desired and wholly alive was like. Above all, he taught her she'd never known intimacy. This—this was intimacy.

When he finally thrust into her, his potency filling her beyond capacity, stroking her through to her soul, she had no power left to even cry out her welcome, just lay beneath him, loving him with adoring eyes and feather-weak caresses, enduring the heart-stopping pleasure in silence, convulsing helplessly to the involuntary wild rhythms of one devastating climax after another, weeping in ecstasy when she felt his violent release inside her.

Then she slept. All morning. Her earlier theory proved correct. He was so comfortable to sleep on. And then she woke up, and it was her turn to explore, savor, study…

"Daddy, I'm fine." Cassandra looked at Vidal, seeking some kind of moral support in dealing with her father's distress. He didn't give it to her, his impassive eyes turning from hers to the coffee he was pouring. "I saw no reason to worry you since it's all over. I knew you and Mom would react this way, worry yourself sick— No, I shouldn't have let you hear it on the news—I guess I didn't think…"

She paused to suffer her father's deserved admonition, his fierce concern, fidgeting as she once had as a teenager when he'd upbraided her over her irresponsible behavior. How could she tell him she'd just forgotten about him and the world in Vidal's arms?

"Daddy, I'm untouched." Well, in *that* way at least. In the days they'd spent in London, Vidal had touched her, all over, in every other imaginable way. In some ways she'd never imagined, too… *Focus, woman. You're talking to your father and he's asking you about your murdered colleague!* "Yes, a colleague died…" Another ragged tirade. "Yes, two others were severely injured, still have a long recovery ahead of them…" And another. "But *I'm* fine, and the world being what it is today, something like that or worse could have happened to me in a *mall*, for heaven's sake.''

Vidal rose, cup of coffee in hand, leaving the reception area. Sudden anger lashed her. He hadn't even asked her to say hello! Her imp turned into a malicious harpy. ''And Vidal is fine, too, and he's here and wants to talk to you. You must make him tell you how he masterminded the hijackers' downfall.''

Vidal's broad back stiffened, then he turned and prowled back to her, his easy step, his steady gaze deceptive. He resented being cornered like this. Well, tough. He was talking to his foster-father! How could he not want to talk to him? Anyway, her father had asked after him half a dozen times already. She wasn't about to lie to her father and tell him she didn't know where Vidal was.

His eyes were cool as he took the receiver from her and drawled a deep and expressionless, ''Hello, sir.''

As he listened to her father, Cassandra's mind whirled. What was wrong with him? Really wrong? She knew by now he was capable of blazing passion and monumental compassion. But was the first only on a physical level and the second on a general humanitarian one? Was he truly an emotional void where personal-level intimacy was concerned? He had to be. What else explained his attitude towards her father? But if he felt nothing for her father, what hope did she have? She hadn't hoped he'd ever love her as she loved him, but she'd hoped he'd feel *something*, that it might grow beyond the sex. What if he was simply incapable of feeling a thing?

Who was she kidding? She'd take whatever he gave her, without one word of love or commitment, forever. Not that she thought forever was on offer.

''It was as ugly as could be,'' Vidal was saying. ''And it could have easily ended in disaster, with all of us dead, or hostages for life. We were just plain lucky.''

She glared at him, mouthed an incensed, ''Thank you very much!'', marched up to him and yanked the receiver from his hand.

"Don't believe him, Daddy! After the situation got violent when some of our colleagues panicked, Vidal had the situation well in hand. Did you know he speaks Badovnan? And kickboxes? And acts? You should have seen the sniveling act he put on, or when he played dead…"

Her father barked on the other end of the line and she winced. "Yes, we're coming home tomorrow. I don't know when we'll arrive. GAO is sending us a charter plane and we don't know who else we'll be dropping off along the way, so I have no idea when we'll arrive. Tell you what, I'll get to my place, get a good night's sleep, then call you."

She put down the receiver and turned on Vidal. It took one look at his devilish half-smile to defuse her anger, start the chain reaction of need that almost burst her heart with urgency. Surely her heart couldn't withstand that abuse for long? Maybe she shouldn't stick around until it gave out?

Vidal prowled over to her again, his eyes detailing everything he couldn't wait to do to her, gleaming with new ideas. And she knew then. As long as he looked at her like that, she'd stick around. What better way to go than in his arms?

"Still want to go sightseeing London at Christmastime?" He stopped a hair's-breadth away, let her feel him, get his measure, scent his potency.

So he'd closed the subject of the phone call and her father. He'd never talk about the past, would he? Never let her in. He was keeping her to the here and now, in the most superficial compartment of his being, without access to what made him himself, to past experiences or future plans. And, weak fool that she was, she was content with that. OK, not content—just accepting.

Oh, please, the voice of truth inside her sighed in aggravation. *You're just plain grateful, and desperate for him!*

OK, so she was desperate. And she wouldn't think beyond the present again. She'd just take each moment with him, treasure it for what it was. She'd deal with the devastation of a life without him when the time came, and not a second before. He wanted it light and uninvolved? She'd give him that!

She pressed back into him, rubbing her breasts against him, drawing his expected response. Her hands went to his daunting erection, the emptiness inside her throbbing in anticipation. "Nah, I'd rather sightsee *you*—again."

"OK." He took one step away and just started stripping. Button by maddening button, right there in the middle of their suite's reception, where someone from Housekeeping could walk in any second. They'd removed the Do Not Disturb sign, intending to go out.

"Don't stop." Keeping her eyes glued to his every rippling muscle and power-laden move, she backed to the door, panting by now, replaced the sign and came back to squirm at the mouthwatering show. She'd seen him naked before— in fact, she'd hardly seen him anything but naked the last three days—but this way, stripping himself so deliberately, standing there unashamed for her inspection... Unashamed? What had he to be ashamed of? It was a miracle he wore clothes at all, didn't go through life flaunting his perfection and driving poor mortals crazy with lust and envy.

And he was hers. Her lover. For now.

He covered the space between them, pressed her against his arousal until she writhed in his arms, then stepped back again, drawling, his voice a hot throb of pure lust. "Your turn."

Her first inclination was to rip her clothes off and jump on him. Then she remembered something. "*That* you'll have to wait for!"

Vidal watched her disappear into the bedroom, stunned.

He waited. And waited. After ten minutes, he felt more than stupid, standing there in the palatial reception stark naked, embarrassingly engorged and alone.

He was trying to breathe, deflate himself enough to get his zipper up when Cassandra came out again. The zipper almost burst.

He had to be dreaming. He *was* still dreaming of her, of

them, every night, even with her in his arms, even after infernos of every sort of fulfillment. He woke up enacting every flagrant fantasy his dreams had invented.

This was one they hadn't.

Cassandra in the belly-dancing costume he'd bought for her in Casablanca! Music, languorous and exotic, accompanied her advance. Her lush figure was displayed to full advantage by the sparkling wisps of chiffon, her mischievous eyes reflecting its color and that of the glittering beads crowning her magnificent hair and hugging her incredible waist. She glided towards him, twirling and pirouetting, her creamy arms and body undulating in perfect tune with the rhythm, her hips gyrating, her breasts jiggling...

He was panting as if he'd run ten miles, his arousal true agony now. "Just to make...one thing...clear—you are trying to kill me, right?"

Her delighted, voluptuous laughter rang out. "I definitely need you very much alive for the coming performance."

"You mean there's more?" He dropped to the couch. "I should tell you I can't stand much more."

"Poor baby. You'll just have to. Now you've seen me in it, I get to perform the seven veils dance and then..."

He slumped until he was almost on his back. "You don't need to knock my head off. It will blow off on its own!"

Her laughter rose as she came to straddle him, showing him she had no underwear on. "Then I get to take it off..."

He exploded into motion, positioning her over him, unable to bear one more second, growling, "It stays on!" Then he thrust all the way inside her. Then again and again. And she took him, rode him just as fiercely.

The sight of her in that magical outfit, bouncing over him, tossing her beloved hair, her flesh quaking in voluptuous shudders of extreme need, her abandoned cries—too much. He exploded inside her, roaring—his disappointment that he hadn't been able to wait for her, that it was over, and his agonized ecstasy at the most excruciating orgasm she'd ever given him. But as his climax went on and on, and he pumped into her harder until he felt he'd poured his very life essence into her, she bucked, screamed her own mindless, violent release, until she collapsed over him, trembling, spent.

They lay limp, entwined, fused, until the sun went down. Night came and he still couldn't find the controls to his muscles. He found his voice, though. At least a harsh, bass rasp that wavered when he said, "That *was* nearly fatal, you know that? I should register you as a lethal weapon."

"You know you're playing with fire, don't you?" Cassandra gasped, plastered to the wall, spread around Vidal, one breast in his mouth, the other in his hand. For answer he thrust at her core through their clothes, harder.

She gasped louder, wound herself tighter around his hips, giving him fuller access. "You know—my folks—will arrive in a—matter of minutes, don't you?"

He took her words into his mouth, kissed her so deeply she was sure he wanted to extract her soul. "I can make minutes do, if you're game." He kissed her until he had her whimpering agreement, then he dropped her long enough to drag her panties off, free himself. Then she was wrapped around him again and—

The door slammed shut and a clamor of feet and voices erupted in her apartment's entrance area.

"Cassie, honey, we're here."

Vidal jolted away from her so hard she fell to the floor with a thud. Collecting her wits much faster than the staggering Vidal, she snapped to her feet, zipped up her sweater and smoothed down her skirt—she couldn't believe he had her wearing *those*—but didn't have time to do anything more before her family entered her living room *en masse*.

Among the instant chaos of six men and women talking at once, exclaiming in welcome and relief at seeing her and Vidal, and four young children screaming in delight at her table of assorted colored glass baubles, she heard Vidal's smothered Spanish curses as he fumbled with his clothes, kicked her panties beneath the couch, keeping behind her, hiding his state, no doubt. There was no hiding what they'd been doing, though. She instantly saw the knowledge in all six adults' eyes. She also knew they wouldn't comment. Not in Vidal's presence anyway.

After all the hugs and a lot of tears, Cassandra along with her mother, sister and sister-in-law, went to the kitchen to get coffee and the desserts she and Vidal had picked up at Heathrow airport, leaving him with the men and the children. Her sister Amanda and her sister-in-law Sara pounced on her at once.

"Spill, Cassie!" Sara urged.

Amanda warned for good measure, "And if you tell us you and Vidal aren't an item, I'll kill you!"

Her mother laughed. "An item? How quaint. Didn't know your generation still used that term."

"That was for your delicate ears, Mom!" Amanda chuckled.

Cassandra sighed. "What do you want me to say? Didn't you see for yourselves what 'an item' we are when you barged into my apartment?"

"Oh, we didn't see enough, regrettably." Sara gave an exaggerated sigh.

"Just signs that we interrupted something climactic!" Amanda whooped with laughter.

"Door bells are there to be rung, you know. Hell, guys, you nearly gave Vidal a heart attack." Cassandra tried to sound peeved, made a spectacular botch-up of it.

Amanda squinted at her. "We're talking about the same Vidal we all know and don't get at all, aren't we? The original iceberg? Though, come to think of it, he looked pretty volcanic as we came in. Hmm, gotta love a man with hidden depths!"

"Icebergs are all about hidden depths, if I remember correctly," Sara said.

Her mother nodded. "Vidal is complex, that's for sure. Convoluted even. He came to us when he was just fourteen, and though he was exemplary in his behavior, certainly making you lot look pretty bad in comparison—you especially, Cassandra—I never got close to him. He never let me. I think the only person who ever understood him was Arthur.''

"Seems to me Cassie gets him too now!" Amanda winked at Sara and the two women howled with laughter at her *double entendre*.

"Gee, guys, glad to be providing you with such entertainment." Cassandra was really peeved all of a sudden. "But, listen, don't you dare say anything like that in front of him. And I hope you're not going to make more of this than there really is to it. We're just...sleeping together. And only for five days now, so put a lid on it, OK?''

Her rebuff aborted their mirth, their faces falling into such portraits of embarrassment and disappointment that Cassandra almost felt guilty. Almost. It was hard to feel anything when her heart was squeezing drier every moment. Not knowing what to say, she borrowed from Vidal's repertoire and studied her feet. At last her mother finished arranging the coffee and desserts on the trays and turned to her.

"It isn't like you to be 'just sleeping' with anyone, Cassandra. If you decided to give the experience a try, why Vidal of all men?''

"Are you for real, Mom?'' Amanda blurted out. "Have you taken a good look at him?''

"Yeah, the guy has to be the epitome of what women would do anything to 'just sleep' with!'' Sara agreed, then she and Amanda sputtered in embarrassment again at Mavis's severe look.

Cassandra picked up a tray, bent on ending the distressing confrontation, and any future discussions. "If you think I'm out of my mind, getting mixed up with a man like him, though I haven't seen his like yet, you're right. But I was in my right mind when I picked Steve and Daniel and Rick. Dependable, predictable men who on the surface had everything in common with me but who turned out to be as alien to me as fish! I think my right mind has been wrong for a very long time. I'm giving my wrong mind a chance now.

Not that this is going anywhere. In a month's time it'll all be history. So just accept what Vidal and I have at the moment, don't question it, don't expect anything from it, and just be your natural, wonderful selves with him, hmm?''

They all nodded, uncomfortable now, disturbed, serious. Which she didn't want at all. She chuckled, made it sound convincing. ''Lighten up, will you? I'm totally fine with all this. We just survived a horrendous ordeal and it's time to celebrate being alive!''

That brightened them up a bit as they returned to the living room to an involved conversation over the hijacking between the men in her life—her father, brother and brother-in-law, and Vidal. If only he were truly hers...

Stop it. Take it as it comes. One moment at a time.

Vidal rose to take the tray from her, leaned down and muttered in her ear, ''Forgot to tell me they had a key, did you?''

She winked at him and he mouthed ''Later!'' with a menacing smile.

She hugged the sensual threat inside her all through the long evening filled with family warmth and laughter, trying to tell herself she *wasn't* begging there'd always be a later with him...

Meeting Cassandra's family had been, as always, excruciating.

Vidal could have lived with it if it had been only the once. But now he was living—no, staying, he was only *staying*—with Cassandra he was seeing them almost daily. For the full month it took him to resolve the Jet's problems.

Her family were being themselves, continuing their normal pattern of closeness, their eagerness for Cassandra's company augmented by their gratefulness to have her back safe.

And they were being so nice to *him*! So natural and warm and welcoming. Mavis was her soothing, healing self, Amanda her bubbly, makes-you-feel-good-about-life-no-matter-what self, Garret still trying his damnedest to be his buddy. The in-laws and the noisy, aggravating, adorable kids were as bad as the rest, inviting, interested, seeking his closeness. It felt as if they were all reaching out with their unconditional love for Cassandra to draw him in, integrate him into their family. They'd tried to include him before, but it had never been this intense, this agonizing.

It was almost enough to make him run to a hotel, hide there until the Jet resumed its interrupted mission.

Almost.

He couldn't even think of wasting a moment with her, waking up to her eagerness, falling asleep counting her slowing heartbeats as she came down from the heights they'd shot to together. The end would come soon enough. He'd rather die than do anything to precipitate it.

But he couldn't bear being close to her family. Any other man would have been delighted by their acceptance, their unbridled approval. But he knew the truth, had faced it long ago and accepted it. His truth. They were just fooled by the socially acceptable façade he'd spent almost thirty years constructing, they couldn't see the darkness and desolation that was the real him.

He'd always refused Arthur's attempts to draw him into their circle, even when he'd had the privilege of living among them. No matter what he'd made of himself, he wasn't on their level. He never forgot the depravity he'd come from, the stain that had tainted his soul forever. For all their generosity and acceptance, he didn't belong among them. He wasn't only an outsider, an intruder, but an impostor.

Now the renewed vigor of their welcome suffocated him. It underlined how alien he was to Cassandra, how their paths could never do anything but intersect for a brief, transfiguring moment before he continued on his solitary, bleak existence, and she moved on to bless some other deserving man's life.

No, the voice deranged with pain and desperation inside him shrieked. *No other man will have her. I love her. I'd lay my life down for her.*

And what good would his life be to her? The woman who

had such connections, such roots, such stability, when he had none? What could an empty shell of a man like him offer such an emotionally rich woman?

A woman who saw him for what he was, saw what he was good for—a temporary, and purely physical, liaison.

He parked his rented car outside the St James's residence, sat there for a moment, fighting the sickness.

Madre de Dios, why did Arthur want to see him?

He could guess why. Arthur had been the one absent from the daily gatherings. He could guess why that was, too. Arthur was mad at him.

Mad? He should want to kill him. He'd betrayed him, the worst sort of betrayal. And after he'd entrusted Cassandra to him.

Arthur should have known better than to trust his like.

There he was, opening the front door to the only home Vidal had ever known, striding to the gate, coming to meet him and—smiling?

Vidal got out of the car, his heart thundering, his footsteps hesitant as he walked to meet the man he considered to be his true father halfway. Arthur took his hand and tugged him into a tight embrace. Vidal's eyes stung, fogged.

He'd thought Arthur had hugged him that day when they'd first returned because he'd been relieved he'd survived the hijacking, because he hadn't known about him and Cassandra yet. But he was hugging him again now… Vidal's legs almost gave way.

"Come inside, Vidal." Arthur towed him inside.

Two minutes later he was in Arthur's study, sitting on the same couch he'd sat on that day Arthur had gotten him out of the juvenile correction center and had told him he wanted him to live with his family. He hadn't been able to believe he'd been sincere then. He still couldn't now.

After a long moment of just looking at him, Arthur finally said, "You're looking good, Vidal. Nothing like when I saw you before you went on the mission."

That had been almost four months ago, when Arthur had

asked him to go on the Jet's maiden voyage himself, to look after Cassandra. He'd been at his worst then, almost about to give it all up. Today, heartache and dread and torment and all, he'd never been more robust, felt more alive.

"That's Cassandra's effect, isn't it?"

Vidal wanted to dig a bottomless hole and hide there forever. *Infierno!* Arthur was telling him he knew what he and Cassandra did together every day. Well, of course he did, *el idiota.* And there was no point in dodging such a blunt question. He exhaled heavily. "Yes, sir."

"For crying out loud, Vidal! When will you stop calling me 'sir'?"

"Never, I guess."

"This was one thing I never understood. Why, Vidal? Why didn't you ever call me Dad as I asked, Arthur at least?"

"Dad was always out of the question. And you're Arthur in my mind, I just can't say it out loud."

Arthur shook his head. "I never understood why you treated me as if we were in some army and I was your superior officer instead of your foster-father."

Vidal looked at the white-haired man he loved with all his heart, who had so much of the woman he loved with all his being. Words that had been simmering inside him for a long time finally made their way to his lips. "You were—are my superior officer, sir. My mentor, my savior—you're just about everything to me. Before you I was nothing, treated as if I was less than nothing. I entered your home to steal, I held a gun to your head, I could have killed you…"

Arthur's blue eyes misted, with—surprise? Vidal had never told him what he meant to him. Not in words. The older man finally shook his head. "No you couldn't have, Vidal. You don't have it in you to be a killer. No matter what."

"Oh, you're wrong. I don't think that hijacker I hit in the head will ever walk again. I saw myself completing the job, choking him, all of them, blowing bits off them and sitting by to watch them squirm and bleed to death.''

''Feeling such rage and hatred was natural, yet you still didn't act on your impulses.''

Vidal barked a harsh laugh. ''Probably because of all those witnesses.''

Arthur shook his head again. ''We'll never know, then, will we? But I *do* know that you'd never harm someone who hadn't harmed you first. That was why, even though you were scared out of your wits when I discovered you stealing, you *let* me overpower you rather than harm me.''

Vidal laughed again, bitter and dismissive. ''You see only good in people, sir.''

''No, I don't. But I saw it in you. I have never seen such a capacity for good as I saw in you, Vidal. You're one of the good guys, the best guys, no matter where you come from, no matter what you think of yourself. I only helped show you your true nature.''

The lump in Vidal's throat was growing, filling his whole chest. He choked around it. ''Is this why you came every day of these six months I spent in prison? Whatever you did it for, you *saved* me. That day I was sentenced, I thought that was it—a string of prison sentences, with a wretched life on the streets hustling in between, until someone killed me. And then you did what I never expected, what no one ever did for me. You cared. You *cared*, sir. Then you went far beyond that. You believed in me. Everything I've ever done since then has been for you, to please you, to deserve your belief. I would do anything for you…''

''Anything but call me Arthur, huh?''

''I called myself that.''

''What? You changed your last name, not your first!''

''My name now is Vidal Arturo Santiago. The Spanish equivalent for Vidal Arthur St James.''

A long, long moment later, Arthur let out a ragged breath. ''Why didn't you let me adopt you, Vidal? Why didn't you change your name to St James for real?''

"Because it wouldn't have been right. I owed you way too much already, sir. The debt burdens me, knowing I can never repay it. I thought I could repay it to the world, if I worked my butt off—but *you*, you're blessed with everything, most of all the blessing of needing nothing. What could I have ever offered *you*?"

"Yourself. I needed more of you than the obedience and the regular reports by phone. I wanted to look at you and take pride in you, wanted you to open up to me. Like now."

Vidal quit trying to pretend he wasn't on the verge of breaking down, let tears fill his eyes, his voice break. "*Madre de Dios*, I'm so—so sorry. I—"

Arthur interrupted his distress. "Don't be, son. I'm just a greedy old man. You gave me more than enough. I'm so grateful for having you in our lives, for all the satisfaction you gave me, for all the time you've snatched from your busy schedule to meet me. And I'm so damned proud of all the good you do. But all that aside, let me tell you this—what you've done with Cassandra..."

Vidal couldn't bear hearing Arthur's disappointment and grief over his betrayal. "Don't, sir, please!" he choked, feeling like scum, wanting to beg his forgiveness, if such a crime could be forgiven. But above all he wanted to reproach Arthur for giving him a test he'd been destined to fail, destroying the only ties that made his life worth living. "You shouldn't have asked me to take care of her. *Por Dios*, I waited all my life for you to ask me something, anything— anything but that! Giving you my life would have been easier. You should have known I'd fail you..."

"You've never failed me, Vidal," Arthur interrupted.

Vidal barely heard him, his guilt and every feeling of inferiority taking him over. "You shouldn't have trusted me. I can't be trusted with her, can't take care of her. I'm too weak, too selfish, too damaged..."

Arthur cut him off again, took him by the shoulders in a firm grip, his eyes firmer, his words final.

"No, you're not. You're everything I want for her, do you hear me? The only one I want for her!"

Cassandra felt she'd never move again.

But she had to move. Out of range of the mutilating truths.

She'd been ignorant all her life. Known nothing of the two men who meant more than life to her.

And, between them, they'd managed to destroy her.

CHAPTER TEN

"MY GOD, Cassandra! You look a wreck!"

Cassandra glared at her father. Vidal had left two hours ago and she finally felt up to facing Arthur without flying into a rage.

She still couldn't help her furious, "Thanks to you, Daddy!"

"Come again?"

Get to the point. Get the facts. "You sent Vidal on the Jet Hospital mission, didn't you? You set me up, didn't you?"

Her father rose, walked up to her, tried to put his hands on her shoulders. She flinched away, shaking with rage.

He sighed. "I already knew he was a major sponsor of the mission, of GAO as a whole. He'd told me he'd lead some future missions, just not the first one. He'd been ill, and I thought it might do him a lot of good if he got out of his funk, changed scenes and routines..."

A sarcastic sob squeezed past the lump in her throat. "Oh, so you advised him to lead that mission for his own good, huh? Not to keep an eye on me? You didn't use his slave-like reverence to make sure he kept tabs on me, took care of the rebellious daughter you think better kept on a short leash and under strict surveillance!"

Her father's shoulders slumped. "I was scared for you, I admit. And it turned out I had every reason to be. I couldn't stop you going, but I was determined you'd at least have the best protection, the best companion. And I *did* think he needed a change. The mission looked better than anything I could have suggested."

"If you'd wanted to stop me from going *then*, all you had to do was tell me he'd be my mission leader!"

"And have you join another aid mission, where I had no one to entrust your safety to?"

She fell to the couch, her head in her hands. "I don't know who you are any more! You lied to me, manipulated me, threw me into Vidal's company in cold-blooded premeditation…"

He cut through her tirade, his voice soft, defeated. "I needed you safe, darling. I needed to know you were with someone I trust, the *only* man I trust. I was so afraid I wouldn't be there for you any more…"

"What?" Her heart squeezed. Everything went gray.

"I had a massive coronary…"

"*No!*" she moaned, then burst into tears.

He rushed to her side, hugged her tight. "I'm fine now, darling. I went in for a bypass two days after you left. I have an excellent prognosis now, and, even if I didn't, I'm over the scare, the desperation."

"How could you not tell me? How could he?"

"Darling, I didn't want to scare you, and no one—"

She could no longer hear him, everything was falling in place in her mind. "That's why you haven't been coming with the rest to our gatherings. You're still recuperating!"

"I'm taking it easy, yes, but I was almost back to normal after six weeks. I've been so lucky."

"Oh, God, Daddy!" She hugged him, a fresh deluge of tears wetting his shirt.

"I'm perfectly all right now, darling. And don't you see what happened? How bringing you and Vidal together was the best thing I've ever done? The moment you were together again you fell in love!"

Cassandra did finally see what had happened. What had *really* happened. She'd seen it when she'd overheard her father's and Vidal's conversation. But, hopeless, hopeful fool that she was, she'd hoped her father's explanations would somehow prove her wrong.

She was right.

Vidal had gone on the mission, was with her now, to repay his debt. Learning about her father's illness must have driven him to extremes to grant him what could have turned out to be his last, and only, request of him.

Now Vidal's early reticence made sense. He'd felt nothing but antagonism towards her then. Since she'd been antagonistic, too, he'd had an excuse not to fall in with her father's wishes.

But once she'd thrown herself at him he must have run out of excuses. The man he'd do anything for had told him to take care of his problem child. Vidal had known his duty. Take the little princess on, any way at all, keep her out of trouble!

But all that passion, it couldn't just have been to please her father! He must want her—physically...

You and a million other available, hungry women!

Yet he wanted her more than ever now. His hunger had been escalating, so maybe he was beginning to feel something for *her*...

Oh? So why did it feel as if he was itching to get away from them all? She'd felt his unease, and it had almost extinguished her soul.

I'm too weak, too selfish, too damaged, he'd said. He hadn't been able to tell her father point-blank that he didn't want to be with her, so he'd tried to paint himself black, had invented all sorts of non-existent shortcomings to make her father think again, even fear for her future with him, so he'd let him off the hook.

But her father knew better, knew his worth and had been adamant in his plans—had refused to grant him his freedom. *You're everything I want for her, do you hear me? The only one I want for her!*

So, itching to get away or not, Vidal wouldn't go anywhere. She now knew he loved her father so much he'd put up with anything for him.

Including a lifetime with her? Oh, God, no.

She would have taken anything Vidal gave her willingly,

honestly. But she would never take a future he'd been co-erced into. She'd die first. She'd leave first.

One and the same really.

Vidal felt reborn. Invincible. High on boundless hope.

Arthur had saved him again. Liberated him. Cured him. He'd finally convinced him that he loved him for who he was, not out of the goodness of his heart. He'd assured him that the demon of violence and madness that had tainted his biological parents and early life hadn't touched him, hadn't left its mark on his soul. He'd absolved him of self-doubt and hatred, once and for all. Vidal could look in the mirror and see a normal human being, not a mask hiding something grotesque. He suddenly felt whole, worthy.

Worthy of Cassandra.

Arthur's assurances had worked their magic there, too. Knowing that the magnificent thing between him and Cassandra wasn't only in his mind, but a tangible, living thing felt by all, knowing that he hadn't betrayed Arthur by loving her, had changed everything.

With every passing second as he neared Cassandra's apartment, hope turned to conviction. Now that *he* believed there was more to him than emptiness and rootlessness, maybe Cassandra would in time see that, too. Maybe she already saw more to him than he believed, needed him beyond the passion and the pleasure.

Maybe she wanted a future with him.

He'd do anything to make her want it, want him. Love him.

As he bounded up the stairs to her second-floor apartment, his eager steps faltered.

It was just that lately he'd been picking up—he wasn't sure what. Same heat, more abandon, but only on the physical level? Something, somewhere had dimmed...

Stop making something out of nothing. You've lost yourself inside her three times since last night. She's been just as lost. It will be all right. It is *all right.*

He opened the door, headed to her bedroom—their bedroom. She was there. On tiptoe, poking something at the top shelf of her wardrobe with a hanger. He took a moment, held his breath and stood still. Watching. Letting her beauty blast his soul. Until he had to have it flay his flesh.

"Mi amor…" He came up behind her, got down for her the small suitcase she'd been trying to reach, turning her, taking her lips. *Can't wait. Can't get enough. Never get enough.*

He'd become an expert at undressing her. More, a magician. Her clothes dissolved in his hands now. If they didn't, they ripped. She went crazy when they did. He wanted her crazy—always—for him. They ripped now.

"Vidal…"

Dios, her voice, his name. He never knew his name could sound like this. Pure hope and security. Passion and insanity. Like now, a throb of fiery crimson satin in his mouth. Any way at all. Could it really be? Could he be *that* blessed?

Suddenly echoes of his name, screamed in pulsing black terror, reverberated through him.

"Cassandra, *mi corazón…*" He pushed her on the bed, face down, flung himself on top of her. Had to hide her. The bullets would hit him on their way to her…

"Vidal!" Her face was turned to him, gasping. He sealed her lips, giving her his breath. She took it, battling with him for more, and he gave it all to her. Her hips arched, demanding the rest of him. He drove into her, filled her, shouted with it, reaching his hands under her to tighten his shield, claim all her secrets, stimulate her into a higher frenzy. *Show me,* mi amor. *Show me how much I pleasure you. Show me how alive you are.*

She showed him, as always, his generous, uninhibited Cassandra. Every time she convulsed around him in the throes of fulfillment it was different. And always better. He'd thought it was the edge of desperation drawing nearer, making him more frantic, honing his senses, making release more explosive. He'd been wrong. Serenity made everything a hundred times better. This time, as he surrendered to the devastating ecstasy inside her, believing she'd be there always, it was the best.

She moved beneath him. He rolled off her, tried to pull her on top of him. But she was rising. He pulled her back, had to have her in his arms, her heart pressed to his, beat for beat. She resisted, pulled away. His heart lurched.

She just wants to go to the bathroom, el idiota. What are you going to start doing now? Smothering her?

She did go to the bathroom. But she could have smiled at him, kissed him first. *Looked* at him.

Dios, what was wrong?

Every doubt and fear and feeling of worthlessness crashed in on him, pinning him down. He lay there, unable to move, waiting for her to come out. Rescue him.

It was almost an hour before she did, gleaming hair scraped off her pale face and back into a ponytail. She was dressed. It made him feel stupid for lying there naked, hoping she'd come back to bed after all that time.

He forced himself up and into his jeans, almost afraid to look at her now.

If something's wrong, I don't want to know.

"So, have the Uzbekistan and Azerbaijan visits been rescheduled at last?" she asked as she started throwing things into the small suitcase.

Was that it? Was she only ready and raring to go? He knew how much she'd loved the work, the mission, how eager to continue the job. Yes, yes—that had to be it.

"Yes. But due to logistical issues, it's going to be for one week only each."

"Soon, I hope?"

"Next Tuesday." He looked at the suitcase, unable to register its significance. "Plenty of time to get ready." *Do it. Tell her. Ask her.*

He stopped her as she reached for her favorite black jeans, held her by the arms, looked into her eyes. Inscrutable. What was she thinking?

Cassandra thought her brain was being crushed. Could almost feel the damage as it happened, the grinding pain that would leave her crippled.

She had to get out of here. While she still could.

"Uh, Cassandra, we need to talk. We haven't had one real conversation since…" His head tilted towards the bed, his searing, heavy-lidded gaze detailing their tempestuously erotic month together.

Yeah, they hadn't been talking lately, had they? An hour ago they hadn't said a word. He'd just grabbed her and even with all the misery and desperation, the humiliation, she'd just begged for him again with every breath.

But what did he want to talk about? Why did he look so tense?

Maybe he'll tell you the truth! Tell you it only started as repayment of a debt…

Oh, Vidal, please!

"I've been thinking about us—and going on from here—and, uh, I was wondering…if you've been thinking too…" He stopped, seemed unable to go on. She'd never seen him anxious before. Now she did.

His eyes roamed over her, troubled, dark. She was certain he'd see only the emptiness that was engulfing her whole being. He wasn't going to tell her the truth. This was some sacrificial speech. Vidal was preparing to throw away his freedom and solitude to settle his debts to the man who'd been his true father. But even with every heroic intention, this was just too harsh a sacrifice.

She had to stop him, save him, set him free.

She moved out of his reach, resumed filling her suitcase. "If you mean going on from here, as in some kind of future…" That cut her. "Then, no, I haven't." And she could say that with conviction. She really hadn't. "And surely you haven't either. Adults have affairs all the time without them ending in some form of commitment. But if you're worrying about what *I'm* thinking, then don't. I don't expect anything from you—I don't *want* anything from you."

Silence. Until she'd finished packing her suitcase. Then she looked up at him. Found his face as blank as a statue's. He was a master at that, the impenetrable bit. No way to know what he was thinking. Probably relieved. Now he could tell her father he'd really tried and she'd been the one who'd turned him down.

She felt his empty stare on her as she picked up her handbag and keys. "Aaron and Arianna have severe gastroenteritis and Amanda begged me to sleep over tonight, the doctor of the family and all that. I tried to tell her I deal in blood and guts, not vomit, but she's at her wits' end. So, just make yourself at home. See you on the Jet on Tuesday."

At the apartment door Vidal's rasp, bass, almost inaudible, stopped her. And she'd nearly escaped! "What about now?"

She pretended to adjust her handbag strap, tangling it in her hair. "What are you talking about?"

"You said you...don't want a future. What about now?"

"Now is as good a time as any to call it quits."

Arthur had been wrong.

And *he'd* been insane.

To think Cassandra could want him. For himself. For ever. For longer, even.

What had he been thinking? What did he have that she could want? Money, status, success? Those might have gotten him most other women. But not Cassandra. And they were all he had. He'd thought he had sex, too. Thought it would give him a bit more time with her.

I don't want anything from you!

Agony. Brutal, annihilating, to a level never even imagined through all his miserable life. He shouldn't survive it. Why did he? Why didn't his heart just burst with it? So he could live with it? He couldn't.

He had to have an outlet. Something. Anything.

Anger. Fury. He could hide there.

She didn't want him because she *couldn't* want him. She'd thrown aside three other men before him, destroyed them, then joked about them. Sex with him had lost its appeal so fast because she was sated, jaded. What he thought earth-shattering was same old for her. A so-called modern woman who approached sex like a promiscuous man. Always ready with protection for the next fleeting encounter. And—and…

None of that was true. It was just *him* she didn't want.

His knees hurt. His eyes burned. He clawed at them, to tear them out of his skull, to stop them burning, found them wet. Found himself on his knees, shedding tears he'd believed he'd been born unequipped to shed.

His only salvation was to hate her.

If so, then he was damned forever.

"I'll be damned!" Ashley exclaimed the moment Vidal went out of earshot. "I'll never understand the two of you. I thought you were keeping it professional, especially after that time back there in the toilet…" She stopped, alarmed by Cassandra's choking no doubt.

"Sorry, Cassandra, but I must ask! What was that all about—again? *He* nearly blew me to pieces. *You* nearly gave me frostbite!"

Cassandra let out a shaky exhalation, trying to stop quivering from head to toe. Being within Vidal's aura, which filled the whole Jet, and this last confrontation…

Only six days remained of the mission. If she survived them.

What was she doing here? Why hadn't she stayed home, picked up the pieces?

Because you want to be near him, under any conditions. Because, after this, you'll never see him again.

Tears rushed to her eyes, right out of her soul. "Ashley, two words—it's over!"

"Dammit, Cass, why?" Ashley looked puzzled, distressed even. No doubt in response to her own distress. "You guys had an amazing thing going."

Yeah. Sure. That was why Vidal had been so relieved she'd ended it. While she, stupid, self-deluding, masochistic fool, had still been praying he'd say something to convince her she'd got it all wrong. Until he'd started those halfhearted attempts to get things resolved so they could remain friends—*friends*!

But just now he'd dropped even the pretense of wanting to be her friend. He'd just finished being the boss, the intolerant, unreasonable tyrant, flaying her at the top of his voice over being late.

"*Two* hours," he'd roared. He didn't care if she'd been looking for a teaset for her mom. No more trips to downtown Baku, for anyone, until the list for the day was done.

That "amazing thing" Ashley had mentioned had to be how other people had persisted in perceiving their relationship as something real.

But Ashley was still waiting for her answer. *Go for the inane. End this.* "These things happen, Ashley."

Ashley got the message, exhaled heavily. "If you need an ear…"

Cassandra nodded, rushed away.

She didn't need an ear. She needed a mindwipe. A soul transplant.

"I thought you were interested in learning the DIEP flap technique, Cassandra!"

Cassandra turned distracted eyes to him and Vidal almost roared.

He sank his teeth into his tongue. *Control yourself. You did enough roaring yesterday.*

But now he didn't only want to roar, he wanted to toss Joseph outside the Jet, stand there and watch him tumble all the way to the ground, preferably breaking every limb in the process! And that was because Joseph was a good friend. He would have wanted to kill any other man.

Cassandra had gone out with him yesterday. Was laughing with him now. She'd replaced him already. *Dios*, that was fast!

Nine days. And during that time, apart from the necessary

conversations over work, she'd been treating him as if he were transparent!

At first he'd been thankful, had kept totally silent. He couldn't have trusted himself not to explode in anger and agony. Then he'd swung between two extremes. Trying to make her talk to him, if only to tell him she was sorry, that she'd try to remain his friend, and wanting to rave and rant and accuse her of dragging him out of his protective shell only to leave him exposed, exiled—destroyed!

He went to bed every night and lay awake reiterating, *She promised you nothing. She owes you nothing.*

That didn't stop his explosion yesterday when she'd come in breathless, tousled and late, with Joseph almost skipping in her wake.

"What did you say?"

He ground his teeth. She seemed to have cut him out of her existence, no longer registering him. A calming breath, then he repeated his question, sounding more gruff and immature than the first time.

Turquoise eyes widened, looked pointedly at the video camera transmitting the procedure to the local surgeons on board the Jet. "Oh, I'm very interested."

"As long as I have your attention, we'll start." He turned to Joseph, trying to curb the hostility in his tone and failing. "I assume I have *your* attention, too, and that we *can* start?"

Joseph raised both his eyebrows, his eyes filling with potential retorts. Then he just shrugged and said, "All set."

Big of him! If he had Cassandra now, he could afford to be.

Dios, no, he can't have her. This has to be a nightmare... Snap out of it. Work!

He drew in a breath, which got trapped in his lungs, suffocating him. He forced it out, along with words. "The DIEP flap, or Deep Inferior Epigastric Perforator flap, is an improvement on the TRAM flap, or transverse rectus abdominis myocutaneous flap. It's an ingenious procedure that transfers tissue from the patient's own abdomen for breast reconstruction, with the added benefit of abdominal rejuvenation. The main advantage here is that the reconstructed breast is similar to the natural breast in softness and in the way it drapes on the chest. Its advantages over other implant reconstructions are that there is no foreign body reaction or capsular contractures, and that scars fade and tissues soften, improving the reconstruction over time.''

Cassandra was now hanging on his every word. At least he had her interest when he was playing plastic surgeon *extraordinaire*!

''Its advantage over the TRAM flap, which harvests the 'six-pack' muscle of the abdomen, the rectus abdominis, along with the overlying excess skin and fat, is that the DIEP flap spares the muscle. That leaves the abdominal wall strong, with less risk of developing hernias, a shorter recuperation period, and with the accompanying tummy tuck much more effective and esthetic. The blood supply is furnished by microscopic reconnection of the deep inferior epigastric perforator artery and veins at the mastectomy site.''

By now he was talking to Cassandra alone. How pathetic was it that even her pseudo-attention made him feel better? ''This procedure is technically formidable compared to other techniques, needing an experienced microsurgeon, but its success rate is more than ninety-eight per cent.''

Dios, was he actually bragging? This was beyond pathetic.

Well, no one was going to be impressed if he didn't give the surgery his full concentration, get his usual results.

He began harvesting the abdominal tissue, Cassandra providing assistance, instruments and suction. By the time he was shaping and creating the breast mound, his artistic abilities were really at work. Cassandra began to ask questions, spot-on, informed, controversial, making his explanations of the surgery a real teaching tool. And he couldn't resist making the most of her attention. Pathetic.

''Yes,'' he said after her last question. ''There are many maneuvers to make sure the reconstructed breast matches, as much as possible, the opposite mound, many subtle ways of positioning the tissues and folding the flap. Like so…''

She watched his every move in rapt attention and assisted him flawlessly, then she asked, ''How can you anticipate the effects of healing, scar tissue, gravity, and mound shrinkage to limit the need for revisions?''

His heart contracted again. How would he live without her stimulation, her sharpness, her challenge? Her everything?

He cleared his throat. ''These factors vary greatly among patients, and even in the best of cases the patient should expect revisions. What *I* can do is make those revisions minimal.''

After that it was a matter of closing the skin, which she did, applying the esthetic technique he'd taught her, as well as and even better than him.

As the video camera was turned off and Joseph accompanied the patient to Recovery, Cassandra sighed. ''I'm glad the poor woman had this opportunity. Her mastectomy scar was *the* worst I've ever seen. No wonder she was so anxious for reconstruction.''

''If she hadn't been, I wouldn't have done it. Patient motivation is the indication here, since it's such a major procedure for purely esthetic gain.''

One auburn eyebrow rose, her expression severe. ''*Purely* esthetic gain? To replace a missing breast and remove a ten-inch-long, two-inch-wide disfiguring scar? It would have to be a man who'd say something like that.''

Where had that come from? ''Now, wait a minute…''

For answer she pushed past him, snatching her disposable surgical garments off and throwing them in the bin. ''Tell me, do you tell your mega-paying customers their operations aren't necessary since they're only for 'esthetic gain', like you told that woman?''

She'd overheard that conversation?

Sudden anger erupted inside him. That she should still doubt his integrity! ''And why did I do that in your opinion?'' he seethed. ''Because she's not paying? Haven't you noticed yet that I'm here of my own free will to perform as many free operations as time allows? And about my 'mega-paying customers'—that is getting so old it stinks. If you want me to apologize for making money, I won't! I had to raise the stakes so I wouldn't be overwhelmed with endless frivolous procedures. Those who could afford it paid for it, and I put their money to good use. I never charged anyone with a real disorder. As for why I thought this woman wasn't a good candidate for reconstruction, it's because she had a huge breast and not enough abdominal tissue to reconstruct a matching breast.''

''You managed it!''

''*Barely*, and she'll still have to reduce her other breast to get an equal appearance. Adding to the revision surgery on this breast, that's probably more than she could afford, money-wise *and* health-wise, as she has a history of cardiac disease!''

''Oh!'' Cassandra's eyes dropped, her color, that flush which he knew covered her down to her toes, that he'd traced with his tongue and lips in long nights of abandon, deepened. Not as much as his distress did. ''I see. I'm sorry, I was out of line…''

She stopped, groaned, turned around and rushed away, walked out of the Jet.

She was walking out of his life in five days.

He had to do something—anything. *Use this.* She was re-acting to him again. Antagonizing him, but still reacting to him. This could be his chance. His last chance.

He caught up with her at one of Baku airport's cafeterias. The feeling of *déjà vu* of her standing in the queue stopped his breathing. Then she turned, saw him, and stopped his heart. As usual. He'd known, with that first look, what she'd become to him. He should have run the other way then, and never stopped running.

No. He wouldn't exchange the torment of loving her for any other bliss.

He approached her, not knowing what to say. What *was* there to say if she didn't want anything from him?

Whatever it was, it had to be rational, calm.

He stopped an inch from her, looked down at her and blurted out, "Are you sleeping with Joseph?"

Heads turned at his loud question. Her only reaction was to pay for her cappuccino and French pastries and head for a table. She put down the tray, turned to him. And slapped him—hard.

Fine. He deserved it. But he still needed an answer.

"Is that a 'no' or an 'it's none of your business'?"

"Is this for your report to my father?" Her color was dangerous now, her breathing ragged. And she was talking nonsense. "If it is, tell him Joseph is a good man and he can rest easy. I'd be *safe* with him!"

Dios, no! If she left him but didn't love another man, he could live forever hoping. But this way—this would be truly the end. No!

Ask her. Beg her. "You'd be safer with me. Cassandra— marry me!"

Her face twisted as if he'd struck her.

He'd thought he'd known despair before. He'd known nothing.

Breathe. She had to breathe. This was no surprise. It had still been a possibility that Vidal would make another attempt to fulfill his 'mission'. So why should it feel like he'd put a bullet through her now?

Because this is the man you were born for, and marrying him should have been your destiny.

And if his offer had been made of his own free will, this would have been the culmination of everything her life was meant to be. But it wasn't.

She opened her mouth to say no and he drowned her voice, his ragged, disjointed. "Don't…just refuse. Take some time. Think. I'll wait—forever if need be. Just don't—don't say no now…"

Was this how people had heart attacks? Strokes? Would he manage to kill her? *Put an end to this!* "We can drop the charade, Vidal. Daddy's fine now."

His stare was uncomprehending, totally confused, as if she'd suddenly started talking a language he'd never heard before. *Remember what a good actor he is!*

"The scare Daddy got when he thought he'd die, the reason for all this, is over. He wanted me to be with the only man he trusted, but he's fine now so we don't have to be together any more to put his mind at rest. I know you'd want to anyway, but this isn't the way to—"

Her words choked when he sagged down, looked up at her in total horror, his face working, out of control. "Is this why you were with me? You were just being Daddy's good girl, hooking up with the man he approved of to please him?"

"It's you who—"

"It makes sense!" His eyes shifted around, his expression dazed as if his sight was turned inwards, pursuing his own realizations and deductions. "You became a surgeon for him. *He* was the man you changed for. He told me how hard you worked to make him proud, thinking I'd abandoned him, thinking to replace me. It became an obsession with you, didn't it? You'd do *anything* for his approval, wouldn't you?"

Suddenly, he exploded to his feet again, enraged. "Tell me one thing! When did you find out he'd be OK, that you didn't have to do *anything* to grant him his seeming last request? That day you walked out on me, wasn't it?"

She nodded, opened her mouth, closed it on a sob when his face crumpled, and for the first time she saw him defenseless. This just couldn't be acting. Could it?

When he spoke his voice was thick and suffocating—in tears? "*Dios*, Cassandra, was none of it real? Did you never give me one kiss, one touch, one *hug*, for *me*? I don't even have any of that of you? I can't even keep my memories?"

He'd just put her own agony into words. She hadn't been able to capture it, to formulate it. Now he had. She'd been feeling she wasn't entitled to her memories since they'd been built on a lie.

"It was premeditated, wasn't it?" he went on, his voice wavering, breaking. "That's why you were already on birth control. You knew you'd have me all over you in no time. So what was the plan? To be with me until he either improved or—or… Then you planned to drop me either way, didn't you? You despise me, believe me soulless, don't you? You thought I wouldn't feel a thing when you did. Or maybe you knew *exactly* what you'd do to me, and loved the idea that you could do *this* to me, see me like this!" He gestured angrily, pointing to his filling eyes. "Has the prank been continuing since that day at Madrid Airport? Am I still paying for not losing my mind and taking you when you were sixteen? Don't you know how close I came to that? How I surrounded myself with bimbos as a shield against you? How long and hard I've hated myself, believing myself a sick monster for even thinking of you? How I exiled myself from your home, how much I suffered in losing that?"

Paralyzed, she watched him wipe his hand roughly over his eyes, smearing the moisture across his cheek, impaling her with his first real hostile look. "I always said you were a tormenting imp. That day at the airport, I thought you'd turned into a fully fledged monster. I changed my mind very quickly—you made sure you changed it for me. But I was right the first time. You *are* a monster, Cassandra."

He was turning away, leaving her. *No.*

"It's *you*!" she shrieked after him.

He half turned, his hard face austere, frightening. Well, he didn't scare her!

"You! *You!* All you said! *You* did it, not *me*! You were the one pleasing my father, the one with the debt that burdens you, the one who'd do anything to repay it. Including taking on your savior's monster child, marrying her even! Don't you dare turn the tables on me. I threw myself at you, but I did it in good faith. I thought you wanted *me*. After that night in the palace I started taking the Pill, hoping you'd act on your desire. *I* lie awake thinking of all our intimacies, knowing that if it hadn't been for Daddy, you would have been having sex with someone else, that maybe you closed your eyes and made believe. None of it was for me. It's *me* who can't keep my memories!''

Vidal turned fully now, stormed back to her, caught her by the arms and almost hauled her off the floor. ''I only touched you when I *stopped* thinking of your father, when I stopped thinking of you as his. When you became only Cassandra, the woman I need in order to breathe. I wouldn't have been able to touch you otherwise. And all the time I was losing myself inside you, I was being cut to pieces, believing I was betraying him, believing I must be the last man on earth he'd want for you. He *never* asked me to take you on. I never knew he was ill. Is he really all right now? What was wrong with him? Are you sure he's all right? I'll run every test there is on him the moment we set foot in the States—no, we'll go back now! *Madre de Dios*, woman, how dare you not tell me he was ill?''

''Because I didn't know! I found out that day. I found out everything that day. Your real past, the magnitude of your love for my father, your feeling of indebtedness, my stupidity… *The woman you need in order to breathe*?''

Everything he'd said hit like a meteor shower, blasting away all the fog and fear and pain. He hadn't been with her because of who she was…but in spite of it.

That meant— *Oh!*

''Yes!''

''Yes, what?''

''I'll marry you. Now! As soon as we get home.''

''Cassandra, if this is another trick…''

''Sure. I'll marry you, make love with you every day, bear your children, love you till death do us part, and then spring on you one day forty years from now and say, 'Fooled ya!'?''

He sagged down again, dropped his head in his hands, his chest and back heaving. She ran to him, contained him in a fierce hug.

"Just give me a minute here," he said raggedly.

Tears were a stream down her cheeks now. Unbelievable elation, but with trepidation tinging it. Didn't he believe her?

He finally raised reddened eyes to her, the silver eclipsed by so much emotion—so much! Her greatest insecurity had been being unable to read his emotions, until she'd believed he didn't have any. His life had taught him to wield opacity as a shield, and he'd wielded it with mastery. Now he'd suddenly dropped it, and what she saw awed her. Vidal, letting her into his soul, giving her the gift of his vulnerability and need. Nothing would ever compare.

"I'm sorry I asked you to marry me."

Oh, no, he wasn't doing that to her. *He wasn't!*

"Is this a counter-prank for my supposed one?"

"*Dios*, prank! This is the most awful thing I've ever had to do, but I must do it. Cassandra, you shouldn't even consider my feelings. Think only of yourself. I'm no bargain. I'm twelve years older than you…"

"Eleven and two months!"

"Oh, all right. It still makes me almost from another generation, not to mention that I come from another world. From hell. Your father convinced me I haven't manifested any of my biological parents' aberrations, but I still carry all their flaws in my genes. What if I transmit them to my children—*if* I can have children? Children I'd be over forty years older than, and almost sixty when they're in high school? On the personal level, I'm a workaholic and, as I found out with you, a sexaholic, too…"

"Is that all, or does your list of reasons not to marry you go on?"

"Those are the main points, but each has so many ramifications…"

"If you don't love me…"

"Don't love you? There's no air in the world without you, *mi corazón*, no taste or sound or sight. No reason for anything. I depend on you, on knowing you're alive and well, to exist. You've always jolted my senses to maximum, stimulated me to the point of pain. I was addicted to you even when you were a brat with rioting curls or pink hair and horrible black contact lenses. You scared the hell out of me with what you made me feel. You were so much temptation that I had to run and never look back before I did something unforgivable. I can't run any more. I'm yours, *mi vida*. The whole conflicted, flawed package. And it's why I'm advising *you* to run for your life. I'm afraid I'll overwhelm you, *mi amor*."

Her lips devoured his words, his love, showing him that her love was a match and more for anything he threw at her. She'd have a lifetime to prove her claims. "Not if I overwhelm you first! I have my own list, you magnificent dream, you. Apart from the age and background, I'm just like you. Underlining the sexaholic part. Every touch and kiss and scream was for you. *You.* Never before you. And there can be nothing after you. In fact…" she giggled "…I've been holding back—a lot. Didn't want you to think I'm *too* wanton."

"I need your pledge in writing you'll never do that again!"

"Oh, I'll devour you from now on, never fear."

"I'm counting on it."

"You know about the imp I share my body with, but I also have a jumping-to-conclusions and insecurity demon where you're concerned…"

"I'll slay it for you."

"You already have. Oh, Vidal, you are the reason, for *me*. You're the man I was born for, born to love. I knew it when I was three."

His face was everything. Everything was there. Love and awe and pride and relief and longing and lust and trust and elation. And just about everything else. He drew her into an endless kiss that told her the rest.

They heard applause.

"Ah, there *is* a world out there." Vidal rose, took a deep

bow in front of their airport audience, swept her up in his arms and strode to the exit. Their hotel was half an hour away.

An hour later, they were still merged, still panting and kissing and murmuring their relief and pleasure and love and every little inconsequential explanation.

He pulled her over him, stroked her in sweeping motions, luxuriating in her feel, in her love, in being connected, on every level, never to be alone again. "Your father is not only a saint, he's a very astute saint, *mi vida*. He brought us together, knowing this would happen."

"It seems he knows us better than we know ourselves, and knew we were made for each other."

"Think this is some grand scheme? For me to break and enter into your home, for your father to catch me, then take me in, so I could be part of your life?"

"I don't doubt it for a second. It's destiny. Our destiny, my love."

"We're so lucky, *mi amor*, for both of us to get Arthur as a father."

"You called him Arthur!"

"Never to his ears, *querida*."

"Oh, it *will* reach his ears, via me."

He pounced on her, caught her beneath him, felt her already melting. "I see I have to overwhelm you to guarantee your silence!"

She met his kiss halfway and straddled him, her heart bursting with wonder at all he was, with gratitude for the blessing of having him. As she met his stroke into her and rode it, she moaned, "We must agree—to take turns—overwhelming each other."

MILLS & BOON®

Live the emotion

Medical romance™

EMERGENCY AT INGLEWOOD by *Alison Roberts*

(Emergency Response)

For Kathryn Mercer and Tim McGrath it was attraction at first sight! But as Kat was off-limits, Tim tried to forget her. Now she is Tim's new paramedic partner in a busy New Zealand fire station, and as they work together the attraction soon becomes overwhelming. Tim knows he shouldn't get involved – but Kat has a secret, and he's the only one who can help her...

A VERY SPECIAL MIDWIFE by *Gill Sanderson*

(Dell Owen Maternity)

Midwife Jenny Carson is the most beautiful woman Dr Mike Donovan has ever seen, and he's determined to break through the shell she has constructed around her. As their relationship deepens it becomes clear that she loves him as much as he loves her – then tragedy strikes and throws their future into uncertainty...

THE GP'S VALENTINE PROPOSAL
by *Jessica Matthews* (Hope City)

Dr Dixie Albright only came to Hope City to solve a family mystery – the last thing she expects is an explosive encounter with a dashing doctor. But GP Mark Cameron has soon won his way into her guarded heart. Now Dixie is at a crossroads – should she put her family's needs first, or should she allow Mark into her life?

On sale 4th February 2005

Available at most branches of WHSmith, Tesco, ASDA, Martins, Borders, Eason, Sainsbury's and all good paperback bookshops.

Visit www.millsandboon.co.uk

MILLS & BOON®

Live the emotion

0105/03b

_Medical romance™

THE BABY DOCTOR'S DESIRE *by Kate Hardy*

(London City General)

When two caring doctors cannot deny — but cannot let on! — that they're attracted to each other, their only option is to have a secret affair. But for maternity consultant Kieran Bailey keeping his relationship with Dr Judith Powell private proves impossible. And if their secret is exposed the consequences will be huge…!

THE DOCTORS' BABY BOND *by Abigail Gordon*

When her stepsister's newborn son is orphaned Dr Andrina Bell doesn't hesitate to step in as his mum. Drew Curtis, country GP and the baby's uncle, wants the best for his nephew too. When he offers Andrina a job and a home she knows she can't refuse. But falling for Drew's charm and kindness in every way — was never part of the arrangement…

THE FLIGHT DOCTOR'S RESCUE *by Laura Iding*

(Air Rescue)

When her ex-fiancé's family offered to buy her unborn baby, Shelly's response was to run! Now, under a different name, flight nurse Shelly is making a new life for herself and her child. But there's something about one of her new colleagues… Flight doctor Jared O'Connor not only makes Shelly's pulse race, he has the same surname as her son's father!

On sale 4th February 2005

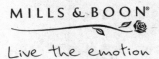

MILLS & BOON®

Live the emotion

His Boardroom Mistress

In February 2005 By Request brings
back three favourite novels by our
bestselling Mills & Boon authors:

The Husband Assignment
by Helen Bianchin
The Baby Verdict *by Cathy Williams*
The Bedroom Business *by Sandra Marton*

**Seduction from 9-5…
and after hours!**

On sale 4th February 2005

*Available at most branches of WHSmith, Tesco, ASDA, Martins,
Borders, Eason, Sainsbury's and all good paperback bookshops.*

www.millsandboon.co.uk

CODE RED

ORDINARY PEOPLE
EXTRAORDINARY CIRCUMSTANCES

CAN SHE
TRUST THE
MAN WHO
SAVED HER
LIFE?

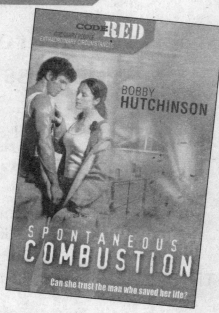

Firefighter Shannon O'Shea enters a burning
warehouse. A beam falls and her path is
blocked. And then a miracle...

Available from 4th February

*Available at most branches of WH Smith, Tesco, ASDA, Martins, Borders,
Eason, Sainsbury's and all good paperback bookshops.*

MILLS & BOON

All in a Day

What a difference a day makes...

CAROLE MORTIMER

REBECCA WINTERS

JESSICA HART

On sale 4th February 2005

Available at most branches of WHSmith, Tesco, ASDA, Martins, Borders, Eason, Sainsbury's and all good paperback bookshops.

4 FREE

BOOKS AND A SURPRISE GIFT!

We would like to take this opportunity to thank you for reading this Mills & Boon® book by offering you the chance to take FOUR more specially selected titles from the Medical Romance™ series absolutely FREE! We're also making this offer to introduce you to the benefits of the Reader Service™—

- ★ FREE home delivery
- ★ FREE gifts and competitions
- ★ FREE monthly Newsletter
- ★ Exclusive Reader Service offers
- ★ Books available before they're in the shops

Accepting these FREE books and gift places you under no obligation to buy, you may cancel at any time, even after receiving your free shipment. Simply complete your details below and return the entire page to the address below. You don't even need a stamp!

YES! Please send me 4 free Medical Romance books and a surprise gift. I understand that unless you hear from me, I will receive 6 superb new titles every month for just £2.69 each, postage and packing free. I am under no obligation to purchase any books and may cancel my subscription at any time. The free books and gift will be mine to keep in any case.

M5ZED

Ms/Mrs/Miss/Mr ....Initials ....
                                                              BLOCK CAPITALS PLEASE

Surname ....

Address ....

....

....Postcode...

Send this whole page to:
UK: FREEPOST CN81, Croydon, CR9 3WZ